Djoser and the Gods

Michael J. Lowis

Stairwell Books //

Published by Stairwell Books
161 Lowther Street
York, YO31 7LZ

www.stairwellbooks.co.uk
@stairwellbooks

Cover design: Alan Gillott, images courtesy Unai Huizi, Denis Simonov, Anastasia Smirnova

ISBN: 978-1-913432-44-7
P3

Also by Michael J. Lowis

The Gospel Miracles: What Really Happened? (2014)
Euthanasia, Suicide, and Despair: Can the Bible Help? (2015)
Ageing Disgracefully, With Grace (2016)
Twenty Years in South Africa: An Immigrant's Tale (2017)
What Do We Know About God? Evidence from the Hebrew Scriptures (2017)
Reincarnation: An Historical Novel Spanning 4,000 Years (2018)
From the Pope to Pigeons; from Dreams to Heaven: Twenty Essays & Anecdotes (2018)
What's it all about, then? Observation on life and the changing times (2019)
Two Mikes and their 39 Stories (2020) (as co-author)

This book is dedicated to those who inhabit other universes. We may not often see them, but we know they sometimes intervene in times of need.

Table of Contents

Prologue

Some scientists believe there are many universes in addition to our own, and that all possible worlds do actually exist. Other boffins disagree with this idea, and maintain that ours is all there is. But one man knew the truth, his name was Neb-er-tcher.

The 'Multiverse' comprises everything that is. Some of the parallel universes within it are far away from ours, but others are very close. Just like bubbles floating in the air, each is contained within its own membrane. These form barriers that normally prevent interaction between them. With an infinite number of universes, the chances are that some will have physical characteristics that are similar to the one we humans occupy. Others are beyond anything we can imagine. Pious folk have given a name to one of them: 'heaven'.

We think we know a little about this divine place where most of us hope to go once we have shed this mortal coil. Hints are given in a range of books that have been preciously preserved, sometimes for millennia. Some believe it operates as a recycling centre, where our souls only spend a short time before being reincarnated back into the world from which they departed. Those who do not subscribe to this idea prefer to think of heaven as a place where we live for eternity in peace and tranquillity.

1

Although Neb-er-tcher did not live in heaven, his domain was far more advanced than ours. The inhabitants had learned how to overcome the constraints of their physical laws, to enable them to traverse space and time. The ability to detect and investigate parallel universes had taken them longer to accomplish, but they had now begun to observe our own world. These peaceful beings were curious to learn more about those who lived on the earth – the only planet they had yet found in our system that contained intelligent life.

Their biological development had in many ways reflected our own, although there was one significant difference. To be sure, at two metres they were a little taller than the average human being, but they had two arms and walked upright on two legs. From the neck down, their skin was devoid of body hair, and was pigmented brown from exposure to the twin suns that circled their world. They had not followed the same evolutionary path as have we, and our primate cousins. It was their heads that identified them as alien.

Although they wished to visit our planet, they would never be able to walk inconspicuously among us. How, then, could they avoid being seen as evil monsters that had come to terrorise the people who lived on earth, and not be struck down before they had a chance to explain themselves? Neb-er-tcher thought he had the answer.

Chapter 1. First contact

We do not know what our neighbours from another universe called themselves, so we shall just have to refer to them as Neb-er-tcherians. They had now been observing us for several of our earth years. Their advanced technology made it possible for them to send signals across the boundaries of parallel universes, including our own. Messages could be received on a planet such as ours but, despite careful monitoring, none had yet been returned to them. They came to realise that two-way communication would not be possible unless a suitable transmitter was available at the receiving end, as well as on their own world.

Neb-er-tcher searched the whole of the earth to see which civilisation was the most advanced. But this was three thousand years before the Christian Era, and our own level of technology was still primitive compared with theirs. China was a possibility, but he eventually decided that Egypt would be the best country for the intervention he had in mind.

Understanding other languages presented no difficulty for his species, as they had developed an ability that can best be described as glossolalia – 'speaking in tongues'. This is not quite the same as occurs in our Pentecostal churches today. In Neb-er-tcher's world it was a universal way of communicating that could either be spoken, or transmitted silently by thought, regardless of a person's home language.

Whilst this was an effective way of conversing among the peoples of his home universe, he doubted that the ability to do this had been developed by earthlings. Nevertheless, he hoped we would be able to understand messages sent to us, even though we did not yet have the technology to respond.

Neb-er-tcher wanted to be the first from his universe to visit earth, so that he could carry out a detailed first-hand study of our culture, but knew he could not do this until the necessary preparations had been completed. It was important that effective communication between the two domains be established first. This would both enable him to keep those in his own world informed of his progress, and make it possible to return home when his expedition was over.

Then there was the matter of his appearance; he would strike fear into the residents if he just arrived unannounced. He needed to be accepted if he was going to interact with the local population. An idea was forming in his mind on how to accomplish this.

His first action would be to try and send a message to the current Pharaoh of Egypt, even though he could not expect to receive a direct reply.

Pharaoh Djoser was ruler over the united kingdoms of Upper and Lower Egypt and, in the third millennia before the Christian Era, he had established his capital at Memphis, on the west bank of the River Nile. His name meant 'strong in arm and speech' and, with his heavy brow and prominent facial features, he was clearly not a man to trifle with. You do not attain and maintain the position of king without being able to win battles and dispose of the opposition.

Like most Egyptians at that time, his skin was dark. He was usually clean-shaven but, on official occasions, he sported the traditional narrow glued-on beard, along with a formal headdress that hung down over his shoulders. His wife, Queen Hetephernebti was there to support him, and his family was made complete by their one daughter, Inetkaes.

It was time for Neb-er-tcher to send his first message, and put his plan for being accepted into practice. Carefully directing his transmission toward Memphis, he said, "Greetings to you, King Djoser. I am Neb-er-tcher, God of the Universe, speaking to you from a land that is both near and far away. Do not fear. I come to guide you, not to threaten you." He could not be sure that the king had heard him, so he repeated the message several times each day over the following week.

Djoser suddenly awoke. Was someone calling me, or did I just have a very lucid dream? he asked himself. Hetephernebti was there by his side, still fast asleep, so it could not have been her. He listened again, but heard nothing so returned to his slumbers. When morning came, he asked his wife, "Did you hear someone calling me during the night? It was very loud and clear."

"No," she answered. "I slept soundly and heard nothing. You must have been dreaming, but I shall question the servants in case they know anything."

The following night the same thing happened, and again on the next. He had to take this voice seriously. Who could it be that can put words right into his mind, as clearly as if the speaker were standing right next to him? It cannot be a mere mortal. The voice had stated that he was 'God of the Universe'. Could this really be true?

Again, he asked Hetephernebti if she had heard anything. "When you asked me before, I told you that I did not, and it is the same now," she replied. "Last time, when I asked the servants, they knew nothing of this, and there had been no strangers in the palace. Do you want to tell me what the voice said?"

"It's been the same message each time," Djoser said. "The man's voice informed me that he was the God of the Universe, and that I had nothing to fear. He wished to guide me. It was as clear as if he was in the same room. Am I going mad?"

The Queen wondered if this was indeed the case, but did not wish to say so. It would be better to humour him, at least for now. "I think you should take this seriously," she commented. "And no, you are not going mad. Perhaps the messages will continue, and you should be ready for something more specific next time."

Neb-er-tcher needed to know if his transmissions had been received, so the next night he said: "King Djoser, there is much that I want to say to you. You cannot yet talk to me but, in order to show that you are hearing my messages, I ask you to do something. Go out into the desert at Saqqara, away from the temple and other buildings, and build the largest fire that you can. Light it when it is dark. I shall be able to detect it."

The Pharaoh, encouraged by his wife, had now become alert to this voice that entered, unbeckoned, so strongly into his mind. He did not need to hear this latest message a second time before acting upon it. The next morning, he firstly related the episode to Hetephernebti. Then he sent for his trusted vizier, Imhotep, and told him what Neb-er-tcher had commanded.

Now Imhotep, whose names means 'he who cometh in peace', was supervisor of everything in the kingdom, and he also had the reputation of being both a magician and physician. Whilst not being tall of stature, his athletic build and confident demeanour identified him as someone who could take charge of a situation and see it through to a satisfactory conclusion.

As a man of action, he avoided the formal robes that he was entitled to wear in his position, preferring instead the practicality of the traditional Egyptian loin cloth. A close-fitting cap usually covered his balding head but, like his master, he shunned the

6

stuck-on beard except on ceremonial occasions. Without him, Djoser would not have been the powerful and successful leader that he was seen to be.

"Imhotep," the Pharaoh said, "I have received a message from Neb-er-tcher, the God of the Universe."

The Vizier looked puzzled. He was used to being the first to know if there had been a foreign visitor to this city. "Your Majesty, by what form did this message come to you? I do not recall seeing an emissary visit your royal residence."

"I did not receive this by the hand of a mortal man," replied Djoser. "The god himself spoke to me as in a dream."

"We hear words in our dreams all the time," Imhotep said, unconvinced. "But we know that they are just products of our imagination."

The Pharaoh was quick to reassure him. "At first, I ignored them, but the words came through strongly night after night. Only I heard them; the Queen did not. I am convinced these messages are real, and that we must act upon them."

Although Imhotep retained some scepticism, he had no wish to openly doubt his master; after all, pharaohs are themselves regarded as decedents of the gods. "What does this Neb-er-tcher wish of us?" he asked.

"His latest message asked us to go into the desert at Saqqara, away from the temple buildings, build a large fire, and light it when it is dark. I am unable to exchange words with him at this time, but he will see the fire and know that we are hearing him."

"Sir, if it is your command, I shall go and collect all the wood I can find and then build a fire in the desert with it," Imhotep replied. "It will take me three days to organise this."

"Very well," said Djoser. "Go and do as you have said. Let me know when the fire will be lit, and I shall come and witness it for myself. I shall then listen for the voice, to hear if Neb-er-tcher has seen the blaze."

With that, Imhotep withdrew to carry out his mission, and the Pharaoh resumed his other duties. That next night, the voice from the God of the Universe repeated the same message, and again the night after that. Djoser wished he could immediately respond and say that the fire would be lit in the next few days, but he knew that at present this was not possible. He was eager to hear what Neb-er-tcher would say to him once he had seen the fire.

Three days later, under the gaze of the Pharaoh and his wife and daughter – for most children enjoy a big bonfire – the ever-efficient Imhotep lit the fire in the desert. The Vizier and his helpers had done an impressive job; it was indeed a spectacular conflagration. Surely the god would not miss seeing this, Djoser concluded. He returned to his royal residence, eager to see if he would receive a new message that night.

Neb-er-tcher ran his bony fingers down the back of his head, smoothing the feathers that evolution had provided there. I have sent the same message for seven earth days now, he said to himself. If I don't see a fire soon, I shall have to conclude that my transmissions have not reached the Egyptian king. Either that, or he is deliberately ignoring them. Perhaps it was unwise for me to say that I was a god; he may see this as a threat to his own authority, or surmise that some devastation will be inflicted on his kingdom should I visit his domain.

It would be night time now on this part of earth, so he took up a position where he could observe the desert at Saqqara. And there it was, burning brightly. He was both relieved and overjoyed. It meant he could now proceed with the next stage of his plan, and prepare the way for a personal journey to the land of Egypt.

Chapter 2. The transmitter

The Pharaoh had tried to stay awake after returning to his palace, hoping that he would receive another message that same night. But it had been a long day; fatigue triumphed, and he descended into slumber.

Suddenly he awoke, sure that the voice had spoken to him again. However, dreams can be very realistic, and he could not be certain that it had been the God of the Universe addressing him. He rested his head back on the pillow, and waited, his eyelids slowly losing their battle to stay open. And there it was again. There was no doubt this time; the voice was clear and strong.

"King Djoser," said Neb-er-tcher, "Tonight I have seen your fire in the desert at Saqqara. I am pleased that you have heard my words, and have elected to respond. Tomorrow, at this time, I shall speak with you once more, and invite you to carry out another task. In the meantime, enjoy your rest."

The monarch slept soundly for the rest of the night, knowing that he would not be disturbed again. As the sun's rays streamed through the window of his bedchamber, indicating the dawning of a new day, he was eager to tell Hetephernebti what he had heard.

"Did you hear any voices during the night?" he asked his wife.

"I felt you moving around in bed a few times," she replied, "but I was not aware of anyone speaking."

"Neb-er-tcher spoke to me again. He said that he had seen the fire in the desert, and was pleased," related Djoser, trying not to sound like a child who had just been given a new toy.

Although she did not like to openly admit it, Hetephernebti harboured doubts about the voices her husband claimed to have heard. Could the pressures of his office be taking a heavy toll on his mental health? She asked him: "Are you sure you were not dreaming? Sometimes these can be very convincing."

"I am confident that the god was really speaking to me," he assured her. "But proof will come to all one day. Neb-er-tcher said he will talk to me again tomorrow night, and ask me to carry out another task. His intentions are no doubt honourable, and we shall surely benefit from his attention at some time in the future."

The Queen did not wish to antagonise her husband any further, so she just smiled and said, "I look forward to hearing what the god will request of you."

Djoser had little opportunity that day to speculate on what the next message would be; he had a country to lead, and there was much to occupy him. There was the constant threat of invasion, so he needed to seek assurance from the commander of his army that the troops were always ready for whatever should befall. There were taxes to be collected to pay for these armies, the food supply chain to be maintained, and the royal residences administered. He did, however, briefly update Imhotep and warn him to expect to be given another task.

When the time came for him to take some mid-day refreshment with his wife, Hetephernebti prudently avoided raising the matter of the anticipated next message, electing instead to limit her conversation to domestic matters. She still wondered if the voices were the creation of his own mind, and was concerned that the constant pressures he was under as monarch were taking a toll on his mental stability.

As the sun dipped below the horizon, the Pharaoh finally ceased his official duties. He could now relax and enjoyed sharing the evening meal with his family. But he was very fatigued after the previous disturbed nights and the heavy workload of the day, and generous quantities of the local wine did little to keep him awake. The urge to retire to his bed and obtain some sleep could not be resisted.

After what seemed to him to be only minutes, but was in reality hours, Neb-er-tcher called him, just as he had promised. "King Djoser, now that I have seen your fire, I know that you will again listen to what I have to say."

The Pharaoh was immediately wide awake, and once more wondered if he had been dreaming. In the dim light he glanced around the bed chamber to reassure himself that he was in the real, familiar world. Hetephernebti was there beside him, still fast asleep. Should he rouse her so that she could confirm that he was fully conscious? No, he would just wait, and listen for the voice to continue – if indeed it did.

And it came again. "I repeat that you must not fear me. When the time is right, I wish to visit your world but, to make this possible, you will need to do something first."

Djoser could not prevent himself from responding loudly, "Just tell me what you wish of me, God of the Universe." His words went unheard by Neb-er-tcher, but they caused his wife to open her eyes.

"What is the matter, my husband?" she said sleepily. "Are you troubled by something?"

"The voice is talking to me again," he replied. "The god says he is going to give me another task to perform. Did you hear anything?"

11

"No," she confirmed, still worried that he was becoming mentally unstable. "But you just carry on listening, and tell me about it in the morning." With that, she resumed her slumbers.

Neb-er-tcher continued with his message. "Although you can hear me, I say again that I am unable to hear you. Before you can talk to me, you will have to construct a transmitter out in the desert where you lit the fire. This is what I have on my world, and it allows me to project my messages through the barrier that separates our two universes."

Djoser wondered what was meant by 'transmitter', and the answer came quickly.

"To build this structure, you will need a large number of stones cut into blocks. These must firstly be laid out in the largest square you can achieve. Then a smaller square of stone blocks is to be built on top of this, and then another, smaller still. These steps must be continued, layer upon layer, reducing in size until they come to a point at the very top."

A pause in the voice enabled the king to reinforce these instructions in his mind whilst they were still fresh. This building project certainly seemed to require much work and expense, but it would all be worthwhile if it meant he could reply to the god, and maybe even eventually meet him.

The message had some further instructions to give. "We call this transmitter a 'pyramid'. The bigger you can build it, then the more powerful it will be. When it has been completed, you will need to dig a chamber underneath the stonework. If your construction is satisfactory, you will be able to go in there and speak to me, and I will hear you. It is also the place where I shall appear to you in person."

This was a long and detailed message, and Djoser hoped that he could remember everything. Perhaps Neb-er-tcher would repeat the instructions, so that he could confirm he had not missed anything. Despite the excitement of this lengthy communication, he soon lapsed into sleep.

When morning came, he gave Hetephernebti a summary of what the god had said to him. After some thought, she commented: "This will be a very large construction project, utilising a lot of our resources and costing much money. Can you be sure that it is not just a clever trick by our enemies, in order to divert our attention so that they can invade us?"

"This is something we must carefully consider," agreed Djoser. "I shall discuss it with my advisers, and we can then decide whether or not to comply with the request. But I am convinced that it will be worth the effort, and that we shall all benefit from the presence of Neb-er-tcher when he eventually visits us."

Once he had finished his first meal of the day, the Pharaoh sent for his five senior advisers. First and foremost was Imhotep, who would carry most of the responsibility for completing the building project, if it went ahead. Then there was Metjen, the Chancellor, who looked after the treasury, and Abraxas the Chief Magistrate. The head of the army, General Intef, was also present, and the final member of this inner cabinet was Nebemakhet, the High Priest.

"Fellow Egyptians," Djoser began, "you will know that, on my command, Vizier Imhotep lit a large fire in the desert. What you may not know is that I have been receiving messages from a being called Neb-er-tcher, who lives in another universe. He asked me to do this so that he could confirm I had heard his voice."

The group members had maintained a respectful silence up to this point but, on hearing this, nervous glances were exchanged, and some murmurings uttered. It was General Intef who spoke first. "Sir, can you be sure these messages did not come from an enemy playing clever tricks, and that they now know you are so far complying with their intentions?"

"I can understand your caution," Djoser replied. "Queen Hetephernebti also showed such concern, but I am confident that there is no evil intention. Neb-er-tcher stated that he was the God of the Universe and that, when all the preparations have been completed, he would like to visit us. I know that our nation would benefit greatly from the presence of such a powerful being."

Intef remained unconvinced by the idea of such a stranger being allowed to enter Egypt, but he chose not to risk antagonising the Pharaoh, who was himself assumed by many to be descended from the gods.

The High Priest was more positive than his military colleague. "My Pharaoh," Nebemakhet began, "if this being from another universe really is a god, then we would gain much from the divine help that he could give us. But you mentioned 'necessary preparations', before he could visit this land of ours. Can you tell us what these would be?"

"It would require a large construction to be built, which he called a 'transmitter'," replied Djoser. "He uses one to send his voice to me, but he cannot hear mine at this time. When we have completed the structure, I will be able to speak with him. He will also be able to use it to transport himself to our world."

On hearing the mention of the need for a building project, Imhotep was eager to have more details. "Sir, can you please tell me just what is required?"

"The god referred to this transmitter as a pyramid, and we are to construct it in the desert at Saqqara where we had the fire. We start by putting together the largest stone square that we can; the bigger it is then the more powerful it will be. On top of this is placed a smaller square of stones, and then a still smaller one above that. This process must continue in steps until the whole structure comes to a point at the top."

"That will be a very impressive monument," said Imhotep. "Our buildings are usually constructed mostly from mud bricks, but this one will require a great number of stones. It will be a big undertaking, and require a lot of work from many people."

Chancellor Metjen was quick to add a comment. "Not only will this take many years to complete, but it will also cost a great deal of money."

"I have taken note of all that you have said," Djoser assured the group. "Before we make a decision whether or not to proceed with this, does anyone have more to say?"

Abraxas, the Chief Magistrate had remained silent up to this point, but now responded to the invitation to contribute. "Sir, I have to share the reservation voiced by General Intef. If this transmitter is constructed, and is successful, we cannot be sure of the intentions of he who calls himself 'God of the Universe' and anyone else who might come through this portal."

"Once again I can understand that caution is needed, and that we need to balance the potential benefits against the risks," replied the Pharaoh. "We can take a decision shortly, but first I need to know if it is indeed possible to construct the pyramid, and whether or not we can afford to do so."

Whilst the others were talking, Imhotep had been thinking about the feasibility of designing and building this structure, and he was ready to state his conclusions. "I shall first have to go into the desert and estimate how large the pyramid will be, and how many stones it will require. My guess is that we can plan to start with a base measuring about a hundred metres square, but this will require countless thousands of stone blocks."

Djoser had a great respect for his Vizier's expertise, but had two questions to ask him. "Firstly, do you think that the building can be completed according to Neb-er-tcher's instruction and, if so, how long would it take?"

"I am confident that we can build this structure," Imhotep replied, "although it will be larger than anything we have done before. We shall have to cut the stone from the quarry at Aswan, and then transport the blocks more than six hundred kilometres down the Nile. These will then have to be dragged from the river to the construction site. Thousands of workers will have to be employed, and it will take perhaps ten or even twenty years to complete."

Chancellor Metjen felt the need to interject at this point. "Sir, as I suspected, this will create a significant strain on our resources. If free citizens are employed, they will have to be paid. Even if we capture slaves to do the work, they will have to be accommodated, and supplied with adequate food to keep them strong and healthy. There will be boats to build or hire to transport the stones down the Nile, and no doubt a lot of other equipment will be needed that we have not yet itemised."

"Do we have sufficient money in the treasury to pay for all this?" Djoser asked.

"Enough to start the work," the Chancellor replied. "But unless we can replenish it with the spoils of war, higher taxes, or increased exports, I am sure the coffers will be empty before the pyramid is finished."

The Pharaoh turned to General Intef. "Are we likely to have any battles where we can benefit from the treasures we loot from the enemy?"

"Sir, as you know we are subject to raiding parties from our foes, but we have always managed to repel them. The main ones are the Nubians from the south, and the Libyans from the west. When we take the initiative and invade them, we capture slaves and pillage their gold."

16

"It appears, then, that we shall have opportunities to supplement our revenues by both peaceful and aggressive means, and gain some slave labour as well," Djoser commented.

Abraxas the Chief Magistrate spoke again. "Although I still have reservations, one benefit from a large building project like this is that it will create employment for many people. Those who are engaged in paid jobs will have less desire to turn to crime in order to survive."

"We must not loose sight of the declared intention of the God of the Universe, if he does manage to visit us," High Priest Nebemakhet said. "Our king has told us that Neb-er-tcher wishes to come to help our nation, not to destroy it. If this means we shall become more powerful and prosperous as a result of his visit, then surely it is worth our investment in building the transmitter."

The discussion continued until all those present had expressed their views. Djoser needed to make a decision, so he said: "Fellow Egyptians, I have heard what you had to say, and it is now time to decide whether or not we proceed with building the transmitter. Yes, there are arguments both for and against, but I think that we shall benefit greatly from Neb-er-tcher's visit. He chose our country from among all those in the world, and we should be honoured that he has done so. Have all your doubts and fears been satisfied?"

He looked around the room to see if there were any dissenters. Although he had supreme authority to act as he wished, he preferred to first obtain agreement from his key people so that they would perform their duties without resentment. Whether from reluctance or conviction, nobody voiced any opposition to what the Pharaoh had said.

"Then we shall go ahead and build the transmitter," Djoser said. "Imhotep, I give you the responsibility for designing the pyramid and supervising its construction. General Intef, if slave labour is needed, then instruct your troops to conscript the enemy they capture into the services of the labour force. Chancellor Metjen, provided there are sufficient funds in the treasury, ensure that all the expenses are paid for."

He then dismissed the advisers, with the final words: "Go now and start immediately. Keep me informed of the progress and, if any problems arise that you are unable to resolve, come and see me immediately. I am sure that Neb-er-tcher will see when we have commenced work on the pyramid, and will communicate with me again."

Chapter 3. The sign

It was the eighth year of Pharaoh Djoser's reign when construction of the pyramid commenced. There was much to organise. Not only would this be by far the largest building project ever attempted in the world at that time, it would also be the first to be made entirely of stone. Mud bricks, baked hard in the hot Egyptian sun, formed the structure of most dwellings, with the more expensive stone reserved for embellishments, and then usually only for temples, royal residences, and other important buildings.

Three weeks after the decision had been taken to build the transmitter, Imhotep requested a meeting with the Pharaoh. "Your Majesty," he began, "I have marked out a square in the desert, measuring over one hundred metres in each direction."

"Is that the largest pyramid that can be built?" the king asked.

"Sir, with these dimensions, I estimate that it will be more than sixty metres high. It will require one third of a million stones to complete. Nothing of this size has ever been attempted before. If we aim for something even bigger, I doubt it will ever be finished."

"This will indeed be an impressive structure," commented Djoser. "Neb-er-tcher instructed me to make it as big as possible and, from what you say, this would indeed be the largest we could hope to complete."

Imhotep was pleased that his master appeared to have accepted his advice, although he doubted that the king really understood the effort and resources required to carry out this massive project. He needed to place some emphasis on this. "Sir, many difficulties remain to be resolved. I have also spoken with those who have worked at the Aswan quarries in the Nile valley, to assure myself that the vast quantity of stone blocks we shall need can be extracted."

"And are you satisfied that they can?"

"Yes, I am," Imhotep replied. "But it will take a labour force of several thousand men, who will have to be housed and fed. The blocks will then need to be transported to the building site at Saqqara. This will require many ships and their crew for the journey down the river, and more labourers to drag the stones from there to the construction site."

The Pharaoh had obviously now fully accepted the true scale of the operation.

"You will also need a large number of workers to actually build the pyramid, once the stones start to arrive here," he commented.

"Yes Sir, and a camp to accommodate them," the Vizier retorted. "In total, we should start with no less than twenty thousand men. Although this will provide employment for all our citizens who need it, it is certain that we shall also require many slaves."

Djoser was starting to wonder if his keenness to build the transmitter was over ambitious. It would take just about all the resources that Egypt possessed to bring this project to fruition. He would have to consult with his senior advisers to confirm that the necessary manpower and money would be available.

"Very well," he said, "you have researched this proposal well. Continue to make your plans, but I must speak with others to see how much labour can be recruited, and how much money we have

20

to fund the construction of the pyramid. I shall inform you of the outcome."

With that, Imhotep withdrew, and the Pharaoh sent for other members of his inner cabinet. "Fellow Egyptians," he began, "the Vizier has reported to me on what is required for the building project. We shall need at least twenty thousand labourers to cut the stones, transport them to Saqqara, and commence the construction."

Turning to Chancellor Metjen, he asked: "Do you know how many of our own citizens are unemployed, and could be enlisted?"

"I do not have the exact figure, but it will not be more than half the number of men that you require," came the reply.

Djoser now addressed General Intef. "We shall obviously need slave labour to supplement our work force. Do we have sufficient numbers at this time?"

"Sir, as you know, we regularly capture raiding parties. Some invaders are languishing in prison, and can be pressed into service. But we may need to take the offensive and go out to capture some more."

"We also have our own criminal prisoners," Abraxas the Chief Magistrate said. "If it is your wish, those who are fit and able can be made to serve their sentences in service, instead of remaining incarcerated."

"I have heard you all," the Pharaoh said, "and I ask that all available labour be seconded to Vizier Imhotep. All the vessels we can spare, along with any cargo barges that can be conscripted, will be needed to transport the cut stones down the Nile from the quarries at Aswan."

General Intef spoke up. "Sir, Imhotep will not be able to supervise all these workers just by himself. Neither can he be at all locations at the same time. If it is your wish, I shall release some officers from the army to take charge of work parties. My deputy,

Captain Meru, could be placed in command of the stone quarries, and the transportation of the blocks. This would allow the Vizier to devote his efforts to building the pyramid at Saqqara."

"That would be very helpful," Djoser responded. "Even if it is only temporary, it will give Imhotep a chance to train his own supervisors. However, it is important that the army is not depleted, but remains ready for any invasion. We have many enemies who would take advantage of any perceived weaknesses in our ability to defend ourselves."

Having received assurances from Intef that the army would not suffer from the loan of some of its officers, the Pharaoh finally wanted confirmation that sufficient funding would be available to cover the costs of this mammoth project. "Chancellor, you previously confirmed that our treasury is in a healthy state, and that it is maintained through taxes and the spoils of war. The building work will take many years to complete. If our finances start to run low, you must inform me immediately. If necessary, I shall then cut back on the construction."

"I shall certainly keep a tight control on the situation," Metjen confirmed. With that, Djoser brought the meeting to a close, and sent for Imhotep.

After summarising what had transpired in the meeting with his advisers, he said: "You will be provided with all the labour this country can muster, both freemen and slaves. This may not be as many as you would wish for, but it will enable you to make a start on the pyramid. The army officers will be there to help you, until you have trained your own supervisors. As we take more prisoners, these will also be placed at your disposal."

"I am grateful that all this will be provided, and I shall do my best to justify the confidence you have placed in me," Imhotep responded. He did not underestimate the challenges that lay ahead of him. This would be a world first, and he would have to be innovative both in the design and the construction technique. Inwardly he was worried that it may not be possible to complete it, despite the resources that would be placed at his disposal. Nobody likes to fail.

The Vizier's moments of silence had not gone unnoticed by Djoser. "You seem rather pensive," he said. "Is there anything you would like to say to me?"

Imhotep did not wish to appear weak in front of the king. "Sir, there is indeed much to think about, and I need to spend some time working on the design of the pyramid before I can be sure how it will be built. There has been no precedent to guide me."

"I can understand the challenges that are before us," Djoser said. "I have committed the nation of Egypt to undertake this project, in anticipation that the visit of Neb-er-tcher will justify all the effort involved. There will be many who do not agree that we should proceed with this. If it fails, then the wrath will fall on my head as the one who authorised it."

On hearing this, Imhotep was reassured that his master was aware of the unvoiced doubts he was experiencing, and was sympathetic toward them. This was reinforced when Djoser added: "You said that you will do your best, and that is all I can ask of you. You must report to me regularly not only on your progress, but also your difficulties and needs. Together we shall try to resolve anything that stands in the way of a successful outcome. Go now and make a start."

"I shall first visit the stone quarries, taking Captain Meru with me," the Vizier said. "Once the workers have been recruited, accommodation for them will need to be built on the site. I shall then place the officer in charge, and return to Saqqara."

"Very well," said Djoser. "In the meantime, I shall issue a decree instructing all available vessels to be commandeered to help transport the cut blocks. Those that are privately owned will be suitably compensated."

After acknowledging this intention, Imhotep departed. The many thoughts and ideas in his head were jostling for supremacy, but he made an effort to stay calm and focussed. At least he would have time to think on the journey up the Nile with Captain Meru.

Once he was satisfied that the operations at the Aswan quarries were running smoothly, Imhotep returned to the building site at Saqqara. He realised that it would take many weeks before the shipments of stone started to arrive. The first contingent of labourers had been put at his disposal, so he put them to work building a camp for the large number of workers that would eventually be employed.

Rather than wait for the stone deliveries to begin, he decided to commence construction on the foundations of the pyramid, using the traditional sun-baked mud bricks. This would not affect the specified design, as all the superstructure would still be of stone. It would also give him the chance to excavate the central underground chamber where, he had been told, the transmissions would take place.

In order to provide a firm base for what was to follow, countless thousands of the bricks were manufactured, and carefully laid on the hundred-metre square that Imhotep had pegged out earlier. Three months later, the first batch of hewn stones was off-loaded from a Nile barge, and dragged the final fifteen kilometres across the sand to the building site.

If the Pharaoh thought that he would start to see the pyramid rise from the desert in such a short time, he was being unrealistically optimistic. Six months had now passed since he had authorised the construction. To him, this seemed quite a long time ago but, to those responsible for organising and carrying out the building work, it was but the first chapter of a lengthy saga. On his most recent visit to the desert to view progress, Djoser called Imhotep over and asked him for his report.

"Your Majesty," the Vizier began, "there has been much to do, and I am pleased with how much we have achieved. The foundations are now complete, and we are ready to lay the first level of stones. As you can see, we have also provided accommodation for the workers."

Djoser started to feel a little guilty that he may have expected more to have been achieved but tried, not altogether successfully, not to show it. "Yes, you have done well," he said rather belatedly. "Do you have all that you need to avoid unnecessary delays?"

"Sir," Imhotep replied, "as you know, Captain Meru is in charge of the operation at the Great Trench in the Nile Valley. Cutting the stones is a slow process, so the more labourers he has then the more blocks he can cut. He is also limited by the number of barges available to transport them here."

"Then I shall take steps to provide more workers, and commandeer additional vessels for him. Please keep me informed of any other needs either of you may have, so that progress can continue unimpeded."

With that, the Pharaoh returned to his residence. He had now seen for himself the true immensity of the operation. Had he been too hasty in making the decision, and committing so many of the country's resources, especially when all he had to support this was a voice he had heard in his dreams? It was clear that many more years would be required before the building would be completed.

"Has the god been in communication with you again? It has been a year since you last heard from him," Queen Hetephernebti asked her husband, as they were taking their last meal of the day.

This question served only to fuel the doubt that was already starting to invade his thoughts. "No, not yet," he said, trying to make it sound like everything was going well and that, anyway, he had not expected Neb-er-tcher to make contact again just yet.

"You do know that there are those who are not convinced it is right to allocate so much of what we have, to a project that was inspired by a person they cannot see? If the people cannot witness something that will convince them of the wisdom of your decision, then it is possible they may rise up and demand that you be replaced as leader of this great country."

Djoser was starting to feel distinctly uncomfortable. The Queen was obviously more in touch with the mood of the people than he was. As Pharaoh, he had power over all, and his subjects were reluctant to voice their doubts and opposition to his decisions. His wife, on the other hand, was attended by hand maidens who heard the local gossip, and were not averse to passing this on to their mistress. He needed to take what Hetephernebti had said seriously.

"I thank you for your warning," he said. "I shall consult with others tomorrow morning. In the meantime, it has been a tiring day, so let us enjoy our evening meal together."

Was it just a coincidence that the voice was heard again that very night? "King Djoser, this is Neb-er-tcher. I have been waiting until I could see evidence that the construction of the pyramid has begun. Now I have seen the foundations, and that the stones have started to arrive on the building site. I am pleased that you have agreed to allocate resources to this project, but I suspect that not everyone is in favour."

As before, the Pharaoh was awake the instant the message began. Had the god been reading his mind? Did he know that he had been hoping to hear from him again? Was he aware that rumours were circulating that building the pyramid was a foolhardy waste of the country's manpower and money?

The voice stopped. Was that all he would hear this night? But then it started again. "I shall send a sign so that your doubters will be convinced that I exist. Exactly one week from today I shall cause a great storm to occur over the desert at Saqqara. A lightning bolt will strike the very centre of the foundations laid for the pyramid. It will penetrate through to the underground chamber where one day I shall appear."

Djoser's immediate reaction was to be pleased that this would demonstrate Neb-er-tcher really existed, and was not just the product of own mind. But then this awesome display of power may give the impression that the god was intending to use it to dominate or even destroy the nation, once he was among them.

Again it seemed to the Pharaoh that his mind was being probed, as the voice continued: "I do not wish it to be thought that my intentions are evil; my desire is to learn from you, and use my abilities to help Egypt achieve great things. You have my promise that I shall come in peace."

With that the message ended. There was much for Djoser to remember, and he had difficulty resuming his slumbers. When morning came, his first action was to repeat to the Queen all that he had heard. This time she had little alternative but to believe it; the message was quite specific. If the lightning bolt *did* happen as the god had said it would, then any doubts about his existence would be dispelled.

After breaking his fast, the Pharaoh sent for his advisors and informed them of Neb-er-tcher's message. As was the case with the Queen, they had to admit that any concerns they may have had concerning the authenticity of the god would be dispelled, once they had seen the sign. As Djoser was now confident that any lingering uncertainty about the wisdom of his decision would soon disappear, it was opportune to ask for more resources to carry it out.

"Imhotep and his men have made commendable progress with the building project," he began. "However, unless he is provided with more labour and sailing vessels, I fear that it will not be completed within our lifetime."

Abraxas, the Chief Magistrate, was the first to respond. "Your Majesty, all the able-bodied prisoners have already been put to work. Unless more are incarcerated, I have no more men to offer."

General Intef quickly rose to the challenge. "Sir, there have been few raiding parties during the past year. Perhaps we should take the initiative and invade some of the territories outside of our borders. We can then make slaves of those we capture."

Whilst Djoser commended the spirit of this offer, he sounded a note of caution. "Yes, by all means do this, but we do not want to trigger a major confrontation with our enemies. That would only lead to us to divert manpower away from the pyramid building, rather than add to it."

The Pharaoh needed to know if the country's treasury was already suffering from the burden of financing the project. "Chancellor, can we afford to pay for more workers, and build more ships to transport the stones?"

"Sir, at present we are not short of money, but our income is not keeping pace with our expenditure. Unless we can generate more through taxes, or loot from the enemy, there will come a time when we shall not be able to continue."

Djoser needed to think about what he had been told, but it appeared that little could be done to significantly speed up the construction. He neither wanted to bring bankruptcy to the nation, nor precipitate a major war with his neighbours. Rather weakly, he closed the meeting with the comment: "Each of you do what you can to allocate more resources to the pyramid project.

We shall meet at the building site next week to witness the promised lightning strike."

There was growing excitement as the day of the promised sign arrived, and many people had assembled at the desert building site. It was the usual bright sunny day, with a clear sky that gave no suggestion of a pending storm. Mid-day passed, and the weather remained calm. It would soon be nightfall.

The Queen, who was as keen to witness the sign as anyone, no doubt expressed the thoughts of many when she said to the Pharaoh: "It is starting to look as if we may be disappointed today, my husband." She then added, her voice trying to hide worries about their safety, "I hope the crowd does not turn against you for making false predictions."

Djoser was about to answer when, in the fading light, a great wind suddenly started to blow from the west. Angry, dark clouds gathered overhead, and lights flashed within them. Without warning, a great bolt of blue lightning struck the centre of the pyramid foundations. Then another, and yet again, each accompanied by deafening thunder crashes. The people were terrified, believing that this would be the end of the world.

As quickly as it had arrived, the storm left them and the skies cleared. The crowds made their way home; they had seen the sign.

Chapter 4. Set-back

The building work continued, now with a little more conviction after the sign had been witnessed by so many people. Lightning bolts from the heavens might have been rare in Egypt, but they were not unprecedented. That one could have been generated as a natural phenomenon, and that it may have been coincidental that it occurred on the predicted day, was not seriously considered. The god had spoken, and his wishes must be respected.

Despite the enhanced enthusiasm, progress remained painfully slow. The increase in labour and Nile transport had so far been minimal, but the resources of the nation could not be stretched further without risking vulnerability to invasion. After a further two years, the first layer of hewn stones had been laid on top of the pyramid's foundations.

In Djoser's eleventh year as Pharaoh, and the third year of construction, Egypt experienced a crisis. It was Chancellor Metjen who broke the news. "Your Majesty, the season for crop planting has now passed, but the Nile has not flooded and enriched the soil. I fear that it will be a very poor harvest."

The same thing occurred the following year, and again the one after that. The mighty river on which Egypt relied for transport, irrigation, and fertilising the land had ceased to cooperate. Famine raged throughout the nation, and non-essential work slowed or stopped altogether. Instead of cooperating and sharing what food they had, many of the citizens resorted to anarchy and robbery.

The Pharaoh ordered that every available resource must be diverted to food production by all means possible. Some crops could be grown in small plots, watered by hand and fertilised with whatever could be obtained; some could be imported; some could be seized from neighbouring territories by force.

Imhotep requested an audience with Djoser to update him on the building project. "Sir, we had just made a start on laying the second layer of stones, when some of our labour force was taken away from us. It was put to work on the land to help with food production."

"It is most unfortunate that the famine has occurred, but the nation cannot survive without food," the Pharaoh replied. "The pyramid is very important to me, and I believe it is for the whole country. Let us hope that the drought will soon be over, and normal activities resumed. I shall meet with others to investigate what can be done. In the meantime, you will just have to carry on with the labour that you have."

Whilst Imhotep was not happy with the reduction of his manpower, he accepted that there was no alternative. He remained determined to make the best progress he could with the resources he had. Maybe the Pharaoh will be able to take some action, once he had consulted with his advisors.

The next morning, Djoser opened the meeting. "Fellow Egyptians, I do not need to explain the serious situation in which we find ourselves. The Nile has not flooded for several years now, and we are low on food despite the extra efforts we are making to avoid starvation. It is unfortunate that work on the pyramid has slowed; had Neb-er-tcher been here he might have been able to use his powers to help us."

General Intef was the first to respond. "Your Majesty, the situation is being made worse by the behaviour of many of our own people. We have had to allocate some of our troops to keep order amongst the civilian population. If it is your wish, we could travel further afield and try to obtain grain, using force if necessary, but this would leave us vulnerable to invasion."

"No, we cannot risk depleting our army any more," the Pharaoh replied. "We need to find other ways to address this situation." Looking around the room he said, "Are there any suggestions?"

The High Priest rarely spoke out on matters of state, but he had his own views on why the famine had occurred. "Sir," he said, "the flooding of the Nile is controlled by the god Khnum, whose temple is on Elephantine Island at Aswan. We may have displeased this deity, and he is punishing us by stopping the annual flood."

"That is a very plausible idea," conceded Djoser. "We need to find out what we are doing that could have incurred Khnum's wrath."

Nebemakhet was pleased that his words had been taken seriously. "Sir, there is much activity at the quarries near where the god resides, and we are cutting a lot of stone for the pyramid. Are we disturbing him? Have we been taking it for granted that he will always provide for us by causing the mighty river to flood?"

"This must indeed be a possibility," the Pharaoh replied. "What can be done to appease Khnum? I would be very unhappy if it meant we could no longer obtain our stone blocks from the Great Trench."

"Sir, if it is your wish, I shall visit Khnum's temple on Elephantine Island, and see what I can discover that might help to bring an end to the current drought."

"Excellent," said Djoser. "Leave as soon as you can. Take one of the barges on its return journey to the quarries after it has unloaded its cargo."

General Intef spoke up. "I shall write a letter for you to give Captain Meru when you arrive at Aswan, asking him to accompany you to the island, and offer all the help you may need."

"Take what ever action you think is necessary, and report to me as soon as you return," the Pharaoh said to Nebemakhet. With that, the meeting ended.

The sail upriver was helped by the prevailing north-south wind, and the journey to Aswan was completed in twenty days. On arrival there, the High Priest met with Captain Meru and gave him the General's letter. "Tomorrow, when you have rested from your journey, we can sail across to Elephantine Island to see what we can discover," Meru said.

No one had ever seen the god Khnum in the flesh, but some had claimed he had appeared to them in a vision. If the descriptions of him were realistic, then it was clear that, like Neb-er-tcher, he had not followed the same simian evolutionary pathway as had human beings. However, unlike the God of the Universe, this deity was depicted as having the head of a ram.

Early the following morning, the two men stepped off the boat and made their way through the trees and shrubs to the temple. It was obvious that it had been neglected for a long time; some walls had started to crumble, and weeds were growing through the cracks in the paving. "This is most disrespectful to Khnum," observed Meru. "If I were that god, I would also want to demonstrate my displeasure at the way my powers over the Nile were being taken for granted."

"I agree," said the High Priest. "We need to renovate the temple right away. Can you spare some men to carry out this essential task?"

"Indeed, I must do so," Meru replied. "The low level of the river is even hampering our own ability to load the hewn stones onto barges."

"Good," said Nebemakhet. "With sufficient labour, we can make a great improvement in a week or so." He then added, "We must also regularly leave tithes and offerings to the god, and pray to him to resume the flooding of the Nile."

Fortunately the main structure of the temple was still sound, but it took longer than anticipated to clean and renovate it. After two weeks, the High Priest declared that they had done all they could. The two men then placed an offering of food from their limited supply on the altar, and prayed earnestly to Khnum. Captain Meru promised that he would make weekly visits to the island to leave an offering, and ensure the temple remained fit for the god.

With his mission now completed, Nebemakhet took his leave of the officer who had helped so willingly, and joined the next barge destined for Saqqara, complete with its cargo of three great stone blocks. Because of the wind blowing from the north, it was not possible to use the sail. Instead, vessels had to rely on the natural currents of the river as it flowed toward the sea. When the water was still, it had to be towed by labourers walking along the river bank.

When almost a month had passed, the High Priest finally arrived at his destination. Although it was tempting to stop and see how the stones were off-loaded for their final journey to the building site, he dared not delay. The King was expecting him, and he needed to present his report immediately.

"Your Majesty, the temple dedicated to Khnum on Elephantine Island had been neglected for many years. I believe the god was displeased at this, and the fact that he had not been presented with tithes. Thus, he is punishing us by ceasing to cause the River Nile to flood."

"Yes," said Djoser. "We have indeed been taking the flooding for granted, and not paying due homage to Khnum for bringing this about. What action did you take?"

"Sir, Captain Meru has been of great help. We renovated the temple as best we could, and left an offering of food from the small supply that was available at the camp. When all this was done, I led prayers to the god, asking forgiveness for neglecting him, and urging him to resume the annual flood."

"You have done well," the Pharaoh replied. "We must ensure that the temple is always kept in a good state of repair, and continue to offer tithes. Also, our prayers to him must not be neglected. Are you now confident that Khnum will cause the river to flood again?"

Nebemakhet had anticipated this question. "We are now into our summer season, and the waters usually start to rise near the time of the solstice. If the god accepts our plea for forgiveness, and wishes to resume his benevolence, then I believe it will happen on mid-summer's day."

"In that case," said Djoser, "I shall issue a decree stating that all remaining seed corn must be saved, so that it can be used for planting once the flood has subsided and the land has received its much needed fertilisation."

As the High Priest took his leave, he could be forgiven for feeling apprehensive. He had, after all, been quite specific in his views on what had caused the Nile to cease flooding, and the action that should be taken. Had he been too confident in predicting when the next inundation would take place? If he was found to be wrong, would the Pharaoh hold him responsible, with dire consequences? All he could do was pray to Khnum and ask for his help.

It was the day of the summer solstice when workers at the Aswan quarry noticed that the water level was steadily rising, and that they would soon be in danger if they remained at their work place. Captain Meru ordered all the men to retreat to higher ground. This proved to be a wise move as, no sooner had everyone reached a safe vantage point, a great wall of water came rushing down river, and overlapped where they had been cutting stone only minutes earlier.

The flood water continued its journey at a rapid pace, spilling over the banks and into the fields as it went. Seven days later, it reached Saqqara, before continuing into the delta and from there to the sea. In a few weeks hence, when the waters had receded, leaving behind its rich deposit of silt to fertilise the fields, the last of the precious seed corn could be planted.

There was much rejoicing throughout the land, and prayers of thanks were offered to Khnum for his generosity in providing the flood again. As was the case with the bolt of lightning at Saqqara, the possibility of it being a natural phenomenon was not considered. There had been times in the past when the rising waters had been weak or absent, being governed by the amount of melting snow on the mountains further south. No, the people believed, the god had indeed spoken.

It was a great relief to Djoser that, once the labourers who had been seconded to the fields had returned, work on the pyramid would continue unimpeded. He would ensure that due homage was paid to the god of the Nile, even when the stone cutting at Aswan had been completed.

There had been little communication from Neb-er-tcher since he had sent the lightning bolt, but he spoke again whilst the Pharaoh was enjoying his first trouble-free sleep for many months.

"King Djoser," he said, "I have been observing events in Egypt. It will still be many of your earth years before the transmitter is ready. Had I already been with you, I could have helped to restore the river to flood, and thus avoided delays to the building project.

However, I am pleased that you are now able to continue with it to the best of your ability."

The Pharaoh did not need to wonder if he had been dreaming this time, as he had grown confident that the voice he was hearing in his sleep was indeed that of the God of the Universe.

The message continued. "I shall continue to watch your progress. If I have any advice to offer, then I shall speak to you again. When you are near to completion, I shall ask you to enter the chamber beneath the pyramid, and we can test the transmitter to see if it is powerful enough for me to hear your voice. If we are successful, when all is finished I shall then attempt to transport myself into your presence."

All was quiet again. Djoser tried to resume his slumbers, but the thoughts rushing around in his head would not let him. Whilst he was excited that he would eventually come face to face with Neb-er-tcher, that day was still many years away. All he could do was continue to provide all available resources to the building project, and devote himself to other matters of state.

The Nile had resumed its regular flooding, food was again plentiful, and one year followed the next with little variation. Imhotep had devised a system of ramps so that the stone blocks could be hauled up to the higher levels. Once the second layer of stones of the pyramid had been completed, the third was added, forming a smaller square than the one before it. The fourth followed, still smaller, and then the fifth.

By the time the sixth layer with its pointed top was being lifted into place, nearly twenty years had passed. Djoser was now seventy years old. His daughter, Inetkaes, had married the royal priest Itju, and was mother to two daughters. Queen Hetephernebti had remained loyally at the Pharaoh's side. She still did not share her husband's confidence that Neb-er-tcher was who he claimed to be – assuming that he was a real entity – but never voiced her views in public.

As he had promised to do, the God of the Universe spoke again. "King Djoser, I have seen that the pyramid is nearing completion, and it is now time to test its powers. Tomorrow, when the sun is at its highest, go down into the chamber and I shall speak with you. You can then answer me, and I shall tell you if I have heard your voice."

The message was repeated several times that night. The Pharaoh slept very little, excited at the prospect of all the hard work at last coming to fruition. As soon as Hetephernebti was awake, he told her what the god had said. "What are you going to say to him, when your chance comes?" she asked.

"There is much that I need to know," Djoser replied. "I shall ask what he looks like, for he has told us he is different from us. I shall ask him about his home country, and how he intends to help us. I shall ask him when he proposes to visit us, and how long he will stay."

The Queen was unable to suppress a little laugh at her husband's torrent of questions. "Enough," she said, "I just hope you receive some satisfying answers."

Time seemed to pass very slowly that morning, as the Pharaoh travelled the eight kilometres from his the royal residence at Memphis to Saqqara, and the site of what was becoming known as the Step Pyramid. When the sun was approaching its zenith, he went down into the chamber, accompanied by two guards carrying torches to light the way. At first, silence. Then he heard the now familiar voice.

"King Djoser, this is Neb-er-tcher. If you hear me, then speak to me."

It was difficult for the Pharaoh to remain calm, but he cleared his throat and said: "God of the Universe, it is good that this day has come. There is much I want to say to you."

There was silence for a few seconds, which felt like an eternity to Djoser. He was about to repeat his words when the voice said, "I heard your voice. The transmission was not strong, and more work will need to be done on the pyramid before I can risk using it to visit you."

The Pharaoh was both pleased that he was able to speak with the god, but disappointed that the promised visit would be delayed still further. "I have many questions to ask you," he said. "You say that your appearance is different from those who live on earth. What do you look like?"

Again there was a short delay before Neb-er-tcher responded. "You will have the answer to this, and your other questions, when we meet. But now I want to tell you what is needed to improve the transmitter."

Djoser had to accept the need for patience, and said, "Very well, what do you wish us to do?"

"The transmission is weak because the sides of the pyramid are not smooth. You must fill in the steps with limestone so that all the walls are straight from the point at the top, to the ground. When this has been done, we shall speak again. I shall leave you now."

Immediately on emerging from the chamber, Djoser sought out Imhotep, who was still on site supervising the construction. "Sir, we can do what the god has asked," the Vizier said, after hearing what was required. "We can obtain fine limestone from the Tourah quarry a few kilometres to the north."

"This is good," the Pharaoh responded. "We no longer need all the barges that have been transporting blocks from Aswan, so I

39

shall immediately order some of the vessels, and the labourers, to bring the limestone."

Another six months passed, agonisingly slowly, especially for the Pharaoh. Eventually the pyramid was completed. With its smooth coating of white limestone, it gleamed brightly in the harsh desert sun. During the night, Neb-er-tcher spoke again. "I have seen that the transmitter is complete. The time has now come for me to make my promised visit to you."

Djoser emerged from his sleep, not doubting for a moment that the message was real and not a dream. Soon he would meet the god, but when would this be?

He did not have to wait long for the answer. "Exactly one week from today, again at mid-day, go to the pyramid chamber and take others whom you wish to be present. I shall then transport myself to you."

When daylight came, Djoser said to Hetephernebti: "In seven days you must accompany me to the transmitter. Imhotep and my other close advisors will also attend. There we shall meet Neb-er-tcher."

It was difficult to remain calm when such a long-awaited and momentous event would at last take place, but eventually the appointed day arrived. The word that something important was about to happen had obviously spread quickly, as a large crowd had gathered outside the pyramid. Shortly before noon, the Pharaoh, his wife, members of the inner cabinet, and several guards bearing torches entered the chamber.

They did not have to wait long before the god spoke, but only Djoser could hear him. "Answer me, and I shall see if your voice reaches me loudly and clearly."

"We are all here," the Pharaoh replied. "I hope that you will be satisfied with the improvements we have made to the transmitter, and that you will be able to visit us."

"I am now ready to try," Neb-er-tcher said. "Please leave an empty space at the very centre of the chamber."

The level of anticipation was almost unbearable. At first, nothing. Then several brief, flashing images appeared in the middle of the room, and quickly disappeared. Again, nothing. The images started again, but this time they remained steady, eventually forming a complete entity. When it was clear enough to identify, the assembled group united in uttering an audible gasp! They now realised why the god had been so reluctant to describe his appearance.

Chapter 5. Neb-er-tcher

The large, unblinking brown eyes set in his hawk-like head calmly returned the stares of the Pharaoh and his entourage, interrupted only by periodic sideways sweeps of their nictitating membranes. Blue, downy feathers on his face were swept back over his curved forehead forming a crest behind his neck. His obvious evolution along an avian pathway resulted in a not unattractive appearance, but one vastly different from that of the human species. It was understandable that the onlookers should have felt uncomfortable in the presence of such an alien creature, despite him claiming to be the God of the Universe.

Neb-er-tcher's short, hooked beak started to move, and all those present heard a high-pitched but musical voice. "Do not be afraid," he said. "I can understand your apprehension now that you have seen me, but I come in peace."

Although it was obvious that the sound was indeed coming from the tall creature standing only a few metres away from them, his words were perceived not through the ears, but directly within the head. The Pharaoh had already experienced this with the messages he had received during the night-time transmissions, but this was different. He could now hear the bird-like vocalisations, and understand the message in his own language. So, this was true glossolalia.

Djoser needed time to recover from his initial shock before being able to reply, but he now felt calm enough to say something. "Welcome to Egypt, God of the Universe. I am Pharaoh Djoser. It is good to see you after all these years of preparation."

"Thank you, Pharaoh. It has indeed been a long time. I am grateful for all the hard work your people went to in building this transmitter so that I could visit you."

For Imhotep, who had designed the Step Pyramid and supervised its construction, it was a just reward for the effort he had devoted to this project for more than twenty years. He felt proud to be standing there, in the presence of the god that many had doubted they would ever meet. But his sense of satisfaction was about to be rudely challenged.

Neb-er-tcher spoke again. "It is fortunate that I managed to reach you safely. You will have seen that my image struggled to remain stable, and I was nearly lost in cyber-space. The transmitter is not yet large enough, or smooth enough, to operate efficiently I cannot risk returning to my home universe until some improvements can be made. In our early experiments, people were unfortunately mentally or physically damaged because of imperfections in the pyramid."

Djoser believed he should answer on behalf of his trusted Vizier, and the countless others who had sacrificed so much to complete this massive building project. "Sir, this is the biggest edifice that has been built on earth. We cut a third of a million stones, and used thousands of labourers to bring it to fruition. Our treasury is nearly depleted, and we had a famine to contend with. We could not have done more."

"I did not mean to belittle your efforts," the god replied. "Indeed, I am honoured that you should have trusted my word, and devoted all your resources to making it possible for me to be with you now. I shall try to justify your faith in me for as long as

I am with you. On my home world we are more advanced than you are, and undertaking such large projects comes easier to us."

The group were starting to recover from their initial surprise at seeing this God of the Universe, half man and half bird, standing there in the centre of the chamber. Despite the strangeness of hearing both the chirps coming from his beak, and the words inside their heads, he spoke with a convincing sincerity. But was this a form of hypnotism, intended to lull them into a false sense of security?

"Are you now ready to leave this underground chamber and emerge into the open air?" asked Djoser.

"Yes, I have no need to remain hear any longer," Neb-er-tcher replied. "I breathe the same air on my home world as you do here, and I am looking forward to seeing as much of your country as possible. So far I have only viewed images of it through our transmitter."

The visitor stretched out his right hand toward the Pharaoh. His long, pointed fingers betrayed their evolution from the claws of his ancient avian ancestors. "If you agree, let us go out into the sunshine together, joined in friendship, to show those waiting outside that I pose no threat to them."

Djoser tried to hide his initial reluctance to grasp the alien appendage proffered to him. When he did, he received a warm although rather bony hand, in an embrace that has long been a sign of trust and acceptance between people.

Together they led the small party through the passageway toward the exit. Lagging behind the others was Guardsman Theshen. He was carrying the last of the torches and using its light to make a final check to see if any possessions had been accidentally dropped. Satisfied that nothing remained in the chamber, he started to make his way toward the passageway.

Then, in the darkness behind him, flashes of light like the ones that had heralded Neb-er-tcher's arrival began again. Theshen turned, and looked toward the centre of the chamber. As before, incomplete images appeared briefly and then disappeared. Eventually they stabilised and there, standing before him, was another alien being.

The creature was clearly another product of avian evolution, but there were obvious differences between him and the God who had joined them earlier. His small head and beady black eyes resembled not that of a hawk, but of an ibis with its long, curved beak ending in a sharp point. A crest of downy feathers cascaded down the back of the head and over the shoulders. There was also a tail – thin and forked – not one that would have helped this individual to fly.

Theshen hesitated. He was alone with the alien. Would it be as friendly as the one who had joined them earlier had appeared to be? Should he say something, or reach out his hand? The guardsman was no coward, but he knew he was in the presence of an unknown entity. He decided that discretion was called for; he would leave the chamber and inform the officials who would be standing outside.

Slowly and calmly, he turned away and moved toward the exit tunnel, hoping that his lack of aggression would indicate that he posed no threat. He entered the passageway, starting to feel comfortable that he would soon be clear of any danger. But then the creature darted forward, grabbed Theshen by his shoulders, and plunged its sharp beak into the side of his neck. Blood spurted from the ruptured jugular vein.

Despite being severely wounded, the guardsman was a trained soldier. He managed to turn to face his attacker, and tried to thrust the flaming torch he was carrying into the man-bird's face. But the alien reacted quickly, and repeatedly pecked at Theshen's eyes.

Mortally wounded, and weak from loss of blood, he made a final attempt to grab his attacker by its scrawny neck, but his grip would not hold. He fell, never to rise again.

There was great excitement among the gathering throng waiting outside when Djoser and Neb-er-tcher emerged from the pyramid. After recovering from the initial shock of seeing such a strange, hybrid being, any apprehension the people may have had soon disappeared. They could see that the Pharaoh and his party did not appear to have any concerns – they were all walking along quite happily together.

It was only a short distance to where the chariots had been left. After the royal
party and their guest had climbed aboard, Djoser turned to address the crowd that had followed them. "Citizens of Egypt," he began. "We greet the arrival of Neb-er-tcher, God of the Universe, who has come to help and advise us how to grow into an even more powerful nation."

On hearing these words from their leader, the people let out a spontaneous cheer. This was to be a time of rejoicing. Would all wars now cease? Would there be prosperity for everyone, and no more famines? There had been an undercurrent of grumbling about the many years of hard work and resources that had been expended on the pyramid project. Perhaps, now that the big day had arrived, all this would be justified after all.

The Pharaoh continued. "Our guest will stay at the royal residence for a time, and then we shall tour all parts of our country. I ask you to make Neb-er-tcher welcome whenever you see him, and wherever he goes. We shall leave you now, but stay and celebrate this joyful day."

The chariots made their way back to the palace at Memphis, leaving the people behind to enjoy their party. The festivities continued well into the night, but eventually all was quiet.

In the darkness, a figure emerged from the pyramid and slipped away unseen.

Once they had arrived at the Pharaoh's residence, Neb-er-tcher settled into the room he had been allocated. His needs were few, and they could be satisfied by what the palace was able to supply. Although his distant avian ancestors ate mostly the flesh of the small animals they could catch, evolution had allowed them to embrace a more varied diet that included grains and other fruits of the soil. He was thus content to eat much the same food as did the royal family.

One item was obviously to his taste. "What do you call these?" he asked during the evening meal, when offered a bowl containing bite-sized edibles, some red, some yellow.

"They are dates," the Pharaoh replied. "They grow on palm trees, and are one of the staple foods of this country. They can be eaten fresh, or dried and stored for later use."

After tasting some Neb-er-tcher commented, "They are good. I would be happy to eat these during any meal."

It took some time for Djoser, Hetephernebti, and the other Egyptians present to adapt to the way conversations were carried out. To hear with the ears the chirping and other musical noises coming from the alien's beak, but then to ignore them whilst concentrating on the words directly entering the brain, required more than a little practise.

As the dinner was coming to an end, Neb-er-tcher said, "You must tell me what your main needs are, and I shall try to help you."

"There are many of them," the Pharaoh replied. "Building the Step Pyramid has taxed our resources to the limit, and this was not helped by the drought that caused a famine. The River Nile did not flood for seven years, and we had to placate the god Khumn before it was resumed."

"I already have an idea in my mind that may help you to avoid future suffering from such hardships," their guest said. "But it has been an eventful day, and my species needs its sleep just as much as yours does. Let me retire to my room now, and we can discuss this and other matters tomorrow." Djoser had no wish to argue; it certainly had been an unusual day.

The sun had been above the horizon for just two hours when General Intef requested an urgent meeting with the Pharaoh.

"Sir," he began, trying to hide his breathlessness. "There has been a murder at the pyramid. When the guards were assembled for a role call first thing this morning, one of them, Theshen, was not among them. Captain Meru, who has now returned from Aswan, immediately organised a search of the whole area. At first we suspected that the guardsman may be lying drunk somewhere, after enjoying last night's party a little too much."

"And where did you find him?" Djoser asked, when Intef paused for breath.

"We had nearly given up hope of seeing him again," continued the general. "The only place we had not looked was in the pyramid itself. We lit some torches and ventured inside. There, lying in the passageway, was the lifeless form of poor Theshen. His face and neck bore terrible wounds, unlike anything a sword or spear would inflict."

"Did Theshen have any enemies among the other men?" the Pharaoh asked. "Perhaps there had been rivalry over some woman, and another guardsman took the opportunity to dispose of him."

"Your Majesty, this is unlikely. The murdered man was good living, and popular among his fellows. He was never in trouble like that. I just don't know who would have wanted to see him dead."

48

"What did you do next?" enquired Djoser.

"We took the body from where it had fallen, put it on a cart, and brought it to Memphis for burial. I know there will be many here who will want to mourn his passing."

The Pharaoh needed some time to decide what action to take. "You did right to report this to me straight away. We do not welcome the news that there is a murderer on the loose, who might strike again. Please delay burying the body until I authorise it; there may be some clues that will help us identify the culprit."

General Intef departed to carry out his instructions, and Djoser went to find his new guest. "God of the Universe," he began. "After we had left Saqqara last night, one of my guardsmen was murdered. His body was found in the pyramid. It is important that we find out who did this terrible thing. You said you had come to help us. Can you assist us with this enquiry?"

"I shall certainly try," Neb-er-tcher replied. "Where is the body now? I would like to examine it."

"My officer brought it here to Memphis for burial, but I have just asked him to wait until I give permission before confining it to the earth."

"Then let us go together and see what we can learn from the corpse."

They went outside and met with the General, and together they walked to the cart that bore the remains of Guardsman Theshen. Intef pulled back the sheet that was covering the body.

"I have seen many battle wounds, but nothing like these," said the General. "They appear to have been made with a round, pointed instrument. Judging by the terrible damage to his face and neck, the poor man must have suffered greatly."

Neb-er-tcher remained silent whilst he carefully examined the remains. "Indeed, these punctures have not been made by the common instruments of war," he said. "I have seen similar

49

wounds like this before, although they were not inflicted in your universe but in the one from which I have come."

"But how can this be?" the Pharaoh asked. "You are the only being from your world who is with us at this time. Are you saying that you, who came to us in peace, are somehow responsible?"

"I am sad that you should have even thought that this might be so," came the reply. "But no, now that the transmitter has been built, it will be possible for others from my universe to use it. I have told no one that it exists, but someone must have been watching what I was doing, and discovered it."

"Even if this is so," Djoser responded, "why should one of your people want to come and murder those who belong to my world?"

"Unfortunately I have my enemies, and especially one who is jealous of my status as God of the Universe – a role my main rival expected to attain. He is the Evil One, and he now seeks my downfall. I suspect that he may have surreptitiously followed me through the portal, and was seen by your guard. He then made sure that his presence would not be reported."

"We obviously have a fugitive at large – one who thinks nothing of murder," the Pharaoh said.

"Indeed yes, and I regret that my coming has brought this upon you," Neb-er-tcher replied. "I shall do my utmost to rid you of this malevolent being. You must immediately seal the pyramid so that no-one else can use it."

Turning now to General Intef, he said: "Until this monster is caught, I recommend that your guardsmen do not patrol singly, but at least in pairs. It is tragic that you have already lost one of your men, and we do not want another such incident. If the Pharaoh agrees, I suggest you now allow the poor man's relatives to take his body for burial."

What had, up to only a few minutes ago, promised to be the start of a prosperous and productive new era for Egypt, was now becoming a potential threat to national security. Once again, doubts started to invade Djoser's mind about the wisdom of agreeing to build a device that could allow alien beings to enter their kingdom.

"Can we catch this enemy of yours?" he asked.

"He has powers equal to my own, and is very good at evading capture. It will be difficult to track him down, but we must try."

"If indeed this individual is the one you suspect, does he have a name?"

"Yes," Neb-er-tcher replied. "His name is 'Set'. He is the Evil One, the God of Darkness."

Chapter 6. The Evil One

The Pharaoh and his alien visitor left General Intef to carry out his instructions, and walked back to the royal residence. It had not been an auspicious start to the day, nor in fact to the arrival of Neb-er-tcher. The more he thought about what had happened, the more uncomfortable Djoser became. It was time for some serious discussion with this enigmatic alien.

They sat down on the first floor balcony of the palace, where they could see the small crowd that had gathered around Theshen's bloodied, lifeless form. Judging from the weeping and wailing they could hear, it was likely that the poor man's family had now come to take the body for burial. Djoser asked one of the servants to bring a selection of food and drink, to help them both relax before the probing began.

Despite their appetites having been weakened by the scenario they had just witnessed, Neb-er-tcher again seemed to be satisfied with the flesh and grain he had been offered. He did not bite off portions of food and then chew them, as do human beings, for his species did not have teeth. Instead, he used his hooked beak to tear off lumps and then swallow them with little mastication. The Pharaoh did his best to politely avert his gaze from this unusual feeding process.

When they had finished eating, it was time to ask some serious questions. "You say you strongly suspect who the murderer is," Djoser began. "Why is he your enemy, and why should he follow you here? I think you owe us an explanation."

"You are correct. Again I regret that this situation has come about; I did not anticipate that anyone else would use the portal. That it is the Evil One to do so fills me with remorse."

The Pharaoh still needed to concentrate hard in order to listen to the voice in his head, whilst trying to ignore the squeaks and chirpings coming from the mouth of the tall, avian being sitting opposite him. "I accept that the arrival of this unwelcome guest was unexpected," he said. "But what do you know of him?"

"I need to first give you some family history," Neb-er-tcher replied. "My world was created by the Supreme God, Ra. He appointed my grandfather, Geb, to be God of the Universe. The union of Geb and his consort, Nut, produced two sons: my father, Osiris, and my uncle, Set."

The Pharaoh was surprised to hear this. "Your uncle!" he exclaimed. "Is this the same 'Set' you believe followed you through the portal?"

"Yes, the same. I was the only sibling that my father and his consort, Isis, produced. When my grandfather died, Osiris was sickly and unwilling to inherit the responsibility that was offered to him. The title was subsequently passed down to me."

"But surely, your uncle had a claim to the position," Djoser said. "Why then was he bypassed?"

"You are correct in your assumption. Set did expect to become God of the Universe, with no rivals. But, even as an infant he was dangerous and unpredictable. It is said that he ripped himself violently from his mother's womb rather than allow himself to be born naturally."

"Indeed, this uncle of yours does appear to be a callous and intemperate individual, to be avoided at every opportunity," the Pharaoh commented. "Certainly not a good creature to be on the loose in my country."

Neb-er-tcher continued with his narrative. "There is not as great an age difference between us as you might think, especially as the longevity of my species is more than twice as long as it is on your earth. My father was the eldest of the two brothers by many years. I was conceived only a short time after my Uncle Set was born."

"Did you have an amicable relationship with him in your early years?" Djoser asked.

"When we were both young, we used to play together, but the games often degenerated into contests to see who was the strongest, or the cleverest. Yes, the rivalry began early. There were times when my mother, Isis, had to separate us to prevent serious injury being caused."

"And what about when you became of age?"

"Set did not remain in the same part of our land where I lived. He knew that the population there supported me, so he would be the loser in any bid for supremacy. His intention was to convince those living far away that it was I who was the Evil One, and that they should join him in bringing about my downfall. He would then be unchallenged as God of the Universe."

Djoser was puzzled. "You say this Set went away from you, but apparently he has been spying on your activities and has followed you here. Are you sure this is the same individual who is now at large in Memphis?"

"You are right to question this," Neb-er-tcher responded. "But, by the look of the wounds inflicted on your unfortunate guardsman, I doubt that any earthly person was responsible. We have people watching every entry point into the domain where I live, but the crafty Set must have avoided them all and returned unobserved. Remember that we have powers that you have not yet developed on your world; if we can now transmit ourselves across universes, then we can certainly also do so across our own land."

"But why should he come back to you alone, and not with great numbers of others to try and overpower you?"

"Whilst he had a good chance of evading detection on his own, a small army would easily have been spotted. My belief is that he wanted to gather more information about my present activities, so that he could plan the best way of bringing about my downfall. It was just happenstance that he was there when I was making my plans to visit you. He saw his opportunity, and followed me."

The Pharaoh was now becoming increasingly concerned about how events were developing. He said: "It is clear to me that you are in danger whilst you are here. And we who harbour you are also at risk, if what happened to poor Theshen is an example. How many more of my people will die until this matter, which is not of our making, is at an end?"

"Once again I feel much sorrow that this situation has been brought upon you, and I shall be tireless in my efforts to prevent any more deaths among your people. Unfortunately, I cannot risk returning to my own universe using the unreliable transmitter, and Set would be foolish if he tried. I know that it will take time and resources to build a new one, so we are both here for some time to come. With the Step Pyramid securely sealed, at least the Evil One cannot be joined by any of his supporters, so it remains a conflict between him and me."

"What do you suggest we do in the meantime?" Djoser asked.

Neb-er-tcher considered the options for a while before responding. "His intention is to overthrow me; wherever I go, he will not be far behind. I doubt that he will deliberately attack your citizens unless they get in his way. Thus, I suggest that a warning

55

be issued throughout your land, telling people that we have an unwelcome visitor, whom they should neither help nor hinder."

"I shall certainly do that immediately. And what next – do we just wait for something to happen?"

"My purpose in coming here was to visit different parts of your land, and help you to grow in power and prosperity. It is the least I can do after all your effort in building the pyramid, and the troubles now brought upon you. Sooner or later Set and I will meet, and we shall then bring an end to this rivalry, once and for all. He will not remain in Memphis on his own, but will be following where I go, and awaiting his chance to strike."

"But how long is all this likely to take?" the Pharaoh asked. "It will be intolerable if we have to remain in this state of emergency for months, or even years."

"We can try to bring the situation to a climax by setting a trap," came the reply. "I suggest that we embark on the tour of your land, just as we had planned. Set will not be far behind, looking for an opportunity to confront me. If we can be in control of where and when this will happen, we shall have the advantage over him."

"And what if you lose the final battle, and we are left with this evil God of Darkness? We shall surely then be his slaves for ever."

Neb-er-tcher shared the same concern, but did not voice it. He needed to remain positive and optimistic. "His dispute is with me, and not with your people unless they stand in his way. In the unlikely event that he is victorious, he will have succeeded in his mission. He will then wish to return to the universe from which we both came, and become the unchallenged leader."

Djoser was little consoled by these words. "You have already told us that the transmitter we have built is unreliable, and that you could not risk using it for yourself to return. Also, that you suspect that Set will have the same reservations?"

"Yes, but I cannot answer for him. He may wish to take the chance of using the pyramid as it is, or force you to devote your efforts to enlarging it. But eventually you will be free of him."

"It seems that I have little alternative but to follow your advice," the Pharaoh said with some reluctance. "Perhaps we should start our journey tomorrow, and travel to Aswan where the God of the Nile has his temple. You will recall that we spoke earlier about how we are troubled with drought and famine, because sometimes the river does not flood. You said that you may have a way of helping us to resolve this problem. If you can, it will help to restore your reputation as a benevolent god."

Neb-er-tcher agreed and, with that, the discussion came to end. Djoser sent for his scribe to dictate the warning message to be posted throughout the land of Egypt. He then called his senior advisers together, and summarised the discussion he had just had with their guest from another universe.

Although a ruthless murderer was at large in the land, it was important for life to continue as normally as possible. "General Intef, we do not want our citizens to be in a constant state of fear. They will be reassured by the presence of your troops on the streets, so I ask you to schedule well-armed patrols to cover all areas where people live and work. As your men go about their task, they should also warn everyone that, if they see the evil Set, they must not try to apprehend him, but immediately report this to your officers."

Once this had been agreed, the Pharaoh turned to Chief Magistrate Abraxas. "When I have left for my journey to Aswan, Queen Hetephernebti will remain here as Head of State. However, I appoint you as executive officer, to be responsible for the day-to-day affairs of this nation. Work closely with the General, and devote yourself to ensuring that our people go about their daily activities just as they normally do. If you need any money or resources to help you accomplish this, then consult with Chancellor Metjen."

It was now time to discuss the situation with Vizier Imhotep. He had worked so long and hard designing and building the pyramid, but now felt remorse that he was somehow being held responsible for the problems the transmitter was causing. Djoser was sensitive to this, and wished to reassure his multi-talented architect that he maintained only a healthy respect for all he had done. "Through no fault on our part, we are faced with a difficult choice," he began.

"Your Majesty, I regret that the portal I designed is not suitable for the safe return of our visitors from another universe," replied Imhotep. "Perhaps you should appoint another vizier in my place."

"That will not happen," the Pharaoh retorted. "You are the most skilful in the land, and we need you to remain in your position. Neb-er-tcher only asked that the portal be the biggest pyramid we can build, and you created the largest structure that has yet been constructed on our world. It is something to be proud of, and will still be an edifice that visitors will come and see thousands of years from now."

The Vizier was relieved to hear these words of confidence and encouragement. "Thank you, Sir. I am pleased that you wish me to remain in your service. What assignment do you have for me now?"

"One or both of our visitors might perish whilst they are on this earth. If this does not occur, the only way either of them can return to their universe is through a reliable portal. Whilst I am away, I ask you to explore the feasibility of improving the transmitter that has already been built. If this is not possible, then devote your efforts to designing a more powerful one. When we return, I shall ask Neb-er-tcher to use his knowledge to help you with both these options."

"I shall start work on this immediately," Imhotep responded. "You shall certainly have my designs by the time you are back from your visit to Aswan."

Satisfied that he had taken the first steps to address the dangerous situation that had already claimed one life, Djoser spoke again to the head of his army. "General Intef, I would like Captain Meru to accompany the party to Aswan. He knows the area well, and has previously visited the Nile God's temple on Elephantine Island. He must bring with him a platoon of at least twenty, well-armed soldiers, to protect us."

The Pharaoh finally directed his gaze toward the last member of the group, who had remained silent up to this point. "High Priest Nebemakhet, you shall come with us to Aswan. You have visited Khumn's temple before, and you know the way of the gods. Also, I shall ensure that you have many opportunities to talk to Neb-er-tcher during the journey. Find out all you can about the life of those in his universe, what pleases them and what does not, their strengths, weaknesses and vulnerabilities. This may help us in the future when decisions have to be made and actions taken."

Once Djoser was assured that everyone understood what was expected of them, the meeting ended. He needed time to make his own preparations for tomorrow's journey, but he also wanted to try and probe more deeply into the nature of the species to which his two visitors belonged. He suspected that Neb-er-tcher preferred to dine alone, being conscious that his way of eating may be off-putting to his hosts. Thus, after enjoying the evening meal with his family, he invited their guest to join him for a final discussion before retiring for the night.

The Pharaoh summarised the arrangements that had been made for their journey, and then asked: "Do you have any idea of what your adversary will do next? The more we can anticipate his movements, then the better prepared we shall be."

"It is unlikely that we shall see him before he is ready for his confrontation with me. As befits his title, 'God of Darkness', he will hide out of sight during the day. In fact, if any of your men do catch a glimpse of him, their lives will be at risk. Set will not be pleased that his presence has been revealed. He will follow us swiftly on foot during the dark hours, with no need for barge or horse. When he needs food, he will either kill it or steal it. If people try to stop or capture him, their lives will be ended."

The possibility that more of his subjects might perish again caused Djoser to feel both anger and concern at the situation that had so unexpectedly been brought upon them, but he had another question for his visitor. "We have seen from the body of the unfortunate guardsman how Set murders those of our own species, but how can you and your people be killed – are you immortal?"

If Neb-er-tcher's beak was capable of indicating a smile, it would have done so. "No," he said. "Even though we are long-lived by your standards, we are not immortal. But we have developed the ability to regenerate certain parts of our body that become damaged, just like lizards and some other animals can do on your world. However, there are limitations to this. If injuries are severe, or our head is cut off, then we shall die."

"You know that we shall be accompanied by twenty, well-armed soldiers," the Pharaoh said. "Surely, if Set appears and moves to attack you, he will be no match for all these men working together."

"If it were as simple as that, you would be correct," his guest replied. "But it is likely that at least some of them would perish during the confrontation, and Set could then escape before he is overcome. But I remind you again that the target of his aggression is me. He will believe that, if he is successful, he can then return to his world as the unchallenged God of the Universe."

Despite the potential dangers that lay ahead of them, there seemed little point in continuing the present discussion. It was therefore time to make the final preparations for their journey. Djoser gave instructions for two of the soldiers to immediately go to where the royal barge was moored on the Nile, and inform the crew that the vessel must be made ready for its journey to Aswan without delay. The men would also need to charter another boat to accommodate the troops that will accompany the delegation.

Once this had been taken care of, all that remained was for the travellers to obtain some rest in an environment that offered a level of safety and security they would not encounter in the days that lay ahead.

Chapter 7. The journey

Once the first meal of the day had been completed, Djoser, Neb-er-tcher, and the High Priest Nebemakhet set off in the royal chariot for the journey that would take them to the landing stage on the Nile. Captain Meru and the remainder of the platoon followed on their horses, accompanied by four servants from the palace who would take care of the domestic duties on board the barges. Groomsmen also travelled with the party so that they could bring the animals back to Memphis; it would be two months before they would be needed again.

Despite the assurances they had been given that Set would remain in hiding during the day, the travellers could not stop themselves from frequently surveying the terrain to ensure that their enemy was not about to leap out and surprise them. They need not have worried because, in little more than an hour, they arrived safely at the moorings and were then kept busy ensconcing themselves on the barges.

By mid-morning, all the provisions hastily purchased from local farmers had been loaded, and the barges set sail for the three-week journey that would take them up to Aswan. Djoser had a concern that he had not previously considered when the arrangements were made, and went to speak with Neb-er-tcher.

"It is too dangerous for barges to sail when it is dark," he began. "We cannot see to navigate, and there are obstacles in the river to be avoided. For this reason the captains always stop and moor their vessels at night. In our case, this will present the evil Set with many opportunities to attack us during the voyage."

Neb-er-tcher considered situation, and then replied: "Yes, I agree that we will be more vulnerable when the sun is not there to light our way, but we are aware of it now and must take precautions. You wisely instructed the soldiers to accompany us, so you will be able to arrange for extra guards to be posted when we have completed our journey for the day. At the first sign of danger, the whole platoon can be alerted."

Whilst this did not completely placate the Pharaoh, he immediately haled the other barge to come alongside, and called for Captain Meru. After summarising the discussion he had just had with their visitor, he added: "I suggest that we moor the vessels in the middle of the river for the night, to make it more difficult for our enemy to reach us. When we need to buy fresh provisions from the farmers along the bank, only your boat should go there."

"It shall be as you command," Meru responded. "I shall make it plain to my men that they must be alert at all times, day and night. If they see or hear anything suspicious, they must report it to me personally."

Djoser retreated to his cabin so that he could quietly review in his own mind the situation in which he and his party now found themselves. After considering all options, he could think of no other safety precaution that should be taken at this time – other than the extreme measure of cancelling the trip. Nevertheless, he still realised that whatever they did would not prevent the Evil One out-manoeuvring them, and continuing with his nefarious intention to eliminate Neb-er-tcher.

The voyage must go ahead as agreed, he concluded. They all might as well try to relax and enjoy the river trip, and remain optimistic that they will reach Aswan without incident. Once they were there, there would be a mission to complete that should hopefully prevent any repetition of the periodic droughts, and the famines that they caused. It remained to be seen whether or not this expectation would be justified.

𓏜

Set had so far only been seen by one individual, and that unfortunate man had been cruelly despatched before he could report his encounter. The unwelcome visitor was adept at playing the fugitive role, and hiding away until he was ready to strike again.

Just as Neb-er-tcher had suspected, he had slipped away unseen from the pyramid as soon as it was dark, and found a hiding place well clear of the camp site at Saqqara. His only action along the way was to steal a chicken from a brood that one of the residents was keeping in a pen. Once out of sight, he tore the head off the poor creature, plucked out the feathers, devoured as much of the raw flesh as he could eat, and saved what was left for a future meal.

When the sun had dropped below the horizon, and the stars had taken its place, Set left his hiding place and followed the tracks left by the Pharaoh's chariot. His avian ancestry had bestowed upon him excellent night vision, and he was very fleet of foot. Taking care to avoid being seen by anyone bold enough to be out and about at this time, he reached the outer perimeter of the royal residence before dawn.

Again it was necessary to conceal his presence, whilst at the same time permitting him to keep watch on the comings and goings at the palace. He soon found a suitable vantage point in an old, disused building destined for demolition. The following morning he saw the chariots and the soldiers on horseback depart,

64

noting with relish that his old adversary, the God of the Universe, was included in the party. He would rest now but, when darkness came, he would follow them.

Come nightfall, once again Set had no difficulty following the tracks, and he eventually found his way to the barge mooring station. The vessels had already departed, and all he saw were the horses that would be taken back to the palace stables the next day. 'Which direction have they sailed?' he pondered.

His ears then picked up the sound of revelry coming from a mud brick hut near to where the animals were tethered. Yellow, flickering candle light could be seen through the open window. Set silently crept up to the building, and listened. Inside, the groomsmen had purchased a large jug of red wine and were having a party, free from any superiors who could enforce discipline. As is often the case with those who have drunk deeply, the men were oblivious to how loud their voices were.

"He's a weird character, this creature they call Neb-er-tcher, I don't know what to make of him," said one.

"But he seems harmless enough to me," another opined.

A third one spoke up. "He's caused nothing but trouble since he arrived. Look what happened to poor Theshen; he would still be alive if it were not for this so-called God of the Universe."

"Yes, but it was not Neb-er-tcher who murdered him," his colleague retorted.

The argument continued, interspersed with the sound of liquid being poured and noisily quaffed. Then a voice said: "Well, he has now left us for a time, and the Pharaoh has gone with him. There was talk of help being given to avoid drought and famine, so we shall have to see what they get up to at Aswan."

Set had heard what he needed to know: the barges had sailed up river. As there were still several hours of darkness remaining, he would immediately set off and travel as far as he could before daylight forced him to seek sanctuary again.

Once he was clear of the few buildings dotted around the mooring station, he went down to the river and waded through the shallows to hunt for small fish and crustaceans. Hard mollusc shells or protesting marine creatures were no match for the sharp point of his curved ibis beak, and anything edible was immediately swallowed. When he was fully satiated, Set retuned to the river bank and continued his journey at a brisk pace.

As soon as the first rays of light appeared in the east, he continued with what was now becoming his familiar pattern of hiding by day and journeying during the dark hours. His pace was faster than that of the vessels and, toward the end of the second night, he had caught up with the party. Ahead of him, moored in the middle of the Nile, were the two barges. It was too late to take any action now, so he would observe the situation from a discrete vantage point. Tomorrow, he could plan his next move.

The next morning, Set observed the royal party set sail as soon as it was safe to navigate. He knew he would easily be able to catch up with them, so it was an opportunity to rest until he could follow without being seen. Sure enough, half way through the following night he reached the place where the boats were moored mid-river. Two guards were visible on one of them but, otherwise, all was quiet. He decided to take a closer look. Silently entering the water, he swam toward the vessels, the darkness rendering him invisible to human eyes.

As he approached, he heard the guards talking quietly to each other. "This is all very boring," said one. "Nothing is happening; our colleagues are all enjoying their sleep inside, but we are out here with nothing to do."

"Yes, I agree," the other commented. "But we have been given an instruction, and we shall be in big trouble if anything goes wrong on our watch. I'll go below and prepare some food. That should cheer you up, Hannu."

Hannu muttered something that signified his agreement, and sat down with his back against the side of the boat. Set immediately saw the opportunity to reduce the number of soldiers by one. He quietly moved up to barge, raised his arm and grabbed the man by the throat; his long, bony fingers crushing his victim's windpipe so that no sound could emerge.

Deftly pulling him backwards over the side of the boat, he held him under the water until he was sure that all life had ceased. Then, letting the body go, the Evil One retreated to the shore, to seek out a suitable place to hide during the day ahead.

A few minutes later, the second guard re-appeared carrying two plates of food. He looked around for Hannu, surprised that he was not still where he had left him. Calling his name met with no response. A feeling of anxiety was now starting to develop. He loudly shouted his friend's name, only to be met with complaints from the other soldiers telling him to stop disturbing their slumbers. Much as he did not want to do it, the situation had to be reported to his superior, Captain Meru.

As befits an officer commanding, Meru had his own small cabin on the barge. He emerged, rubbing the sleep from his eyes whilst being apprised of the situation. "Are you telling me that that, contrary to the strict orders you were given, you left one man alone on the deck?"

"I am sorry, Sir," the soldier replied. "Hannu was not in good spirits, so I briefly left to fetch him some food from the galley. I was away no longer than five or six minutes."

"But this was long enough for your partner to get himself into trouble," the officer said. "You shall be disciplined for this, but first of all we must find out what happened to him."

They went back on deck. A search of the whole vessel revealed no trace of guardsman Hannu. The other soldiers found it impossible to continue their sleep through all this commotion. Some of them went out on deck to see what was going on, and join in the search for their missing comrade. "Sir, Sir," one of them shouted. "I can see something floating in the water. It looks like it might be a body."

Using an oar to pull the bundle to the side of the boat, they lifted it on board. Their suspicions were confirmed; it was indeed the lifeless form of their colleague, Hannu.

"Was he drunk when you left him?" Meru asked the guardsman. "Could he have fallen overboard?"

"No Sir, neither of us had touched any wine whilst we were on duty. He may have been weary, but he was completely sober."

The officer carefully examined the body. "There are red marks on the man's throat," he said. "It looks like it has been crushed. Hannu's death was no accident; he has been murdered. Everyone on board is under suspicion." Turning now to the other guardsman again, he asked, "Did you have a fight with your companion, strangle him, and then cast his body over the side?"

"I swear I did not," the man replied, his voice now betraying the growing fear that he risked being in far more trouble over this matter than he already was. "Hannu and I were comrades who served together and fought side by side to help defend this nation of ours. I promise you that he was alive and well when I left him to fetch the food."

"Very well," Meru said. "We shall talk again about this matter, but firstly I must report this unfortunate death to the Pharaoh."

Those in the royal barge were starting to wake up and prepare themselves for another day's sailing once it was fully daylight. Captain Meru ordered his men to bring their boat alongside the other one, stepped across, and asked to speak to Djoser. "Your

68

Majesty, it looks like one of my soldiers has been murdered," he began.

"I am most saddened to hear this, but surprised," the Pharaoh retorted. "There are twenty of your men on your barge, and we are safely moored in the middle of the river. One of your own troops must be an assassin."

"Sir, that is what I first suspected. However, I would personally vouch for all the soldiers I have with me. We have fought together side by side in the past, and they are all loyal to the crown."

"Then who committed this crime, if it was not one of your own people?"

Before Meru could reply Neb-er-tcher, who had heard the disturbance, joined the meeting to find out the cause of all the activity. Once the Captain had described what had happened, he asked: "Can you bring the body onto this boat; I would like to examine it for myself."

The order was given, and Hannu's remains were carefully laid on the deck of the royal barge. The God of the Universe carried out a detailed inspection before announcing: "There are no wounds on this poor man, except for the bruising on his neck. If you look closely, you can see several marks on the skin, side by side. I suspect that these were made by long, powerful fingers, not unlike my own."

It did not take long for Djoser to recognise the significance of this statement, and it was quickly confirmed by Neb-er-tcher: "I believe the guard was murdered by the evil Set."

"So he has followed us, and is close by," the Pharaoh said.

"Yes, I think that is the case," agreed his guest. "He killed this unfortunate individual to demonstrate his presence to us. If he sees an opportunity, he will do the same again, even though his ultimate aim is to do battle with me."

Regret that he had allowed the god to transport himself to this world again dominated Djoser's mind. But he could not reverse time, and there seemed little alternative but to see this chain of events through to its conclusion. "We must be rid of this demon as soon as possible. I have already lost two of my men. What can you do to prevent any more of this needless killing?"

"I am indeed sorry that what I hoped would be of great benefit to you and your country has so far achieved nothing but trouble," Neb-er-tcher said. "Now that we know Set is watching us, I suggest you increase your security measures to avoid any more opportunist murders. From my side, I shall devise a trap for the Evil One, so that his confrontation with me will take place as soon as it can be arranged."

The Pharaoh had to be satisfied with this, at least for the time being. Captain Meru had so far remained silent, but now spoke up. "Your Majesty, I take responsibility for not ensuring that adequate guards and lookouts were on duty, both day and night. I shall ensure that this will not happen in the future. Also, with your permission, I shall ensure that poor Hannu is buried with due reverence."

Once the body had been transferred back to the soldier's barge, there was little more to do but to set sail and continue the journey to Aswan.

From his hiding place on the river bank, Set had observed the comings and goings, and the consternation he had caused. It had been a good night for him, he mused. Next time, his target would be someone more important than just a simple guardsman.

Chapter 8. The High Priest

The loss of one of their fellows weighed heavily on the mood of the rest of the party. However, once the strengthened security was in place, there was little alternative but to try and relax during the remainder of the voyage up the Nile. Neb-er-tcher had said he was confident that Set would not attempt to approach the vessels during the day, especially if they kept to the centre of the river.

High Priest Nebemakhet had been asked to accompany the royal party so that he could spend time with their guest, and learn all he could about his character, his background, and the world he came from. It would be more than two weeks before they reached their destination, and there was little to keep them occupied. Now was a suitable time to arrange the first meeting.

Djoser said that he wanted the chats to remain informal, and not make it obvious that the true intention was to gather information that could prove useful at a future date. Neb-er-tcher was seated in the stern of the barge, as the north wind propelled it steadily along. His large, expressive eyes were directed toward the river bank, and the wisps of blue, downy feathers that formed the crest behind his head were gently ruffling in the breeze.

The High Priest saw his opportunity, and approached. The dress code for holy men of the time forbade the wearing of animal products such as leather and wool. Instead he wore the traditional wrap-around skirt made of linen, and sandals woven from papyrus. Around his neck was a collar, and attached to this was a short cape; its blue and yellow horizontal stripes providing a colourful contrast to the plain white of his other garments.

"Are you looking to see if you can spot your adversary," he asked, hoping that this would sound like an innocuous question.

"No, not deliberately," the God of the Universe replied. "But it is simply a strategy we inherited from our ancestors. It motivates us to be constantly on the look-out for danger, wherever we are and whatever we are doing."

Nebemakhet was encouraged that their guest was not resisting his attempts to initiate a conversation. In his own position as the most senior member of the priestly cast in the land of Egypt, he considered himself to be the appropriate person to converse with divine entities. Up to now he had not been given the opportunity to play a meaningful role, so he intended to take full advantage of the chance that now presented itself.

He continued with another question that this time would require a more detailed response. "The Pharaoh has summarised to me what you told him about your early life and relationship with your uncle Set, who now seeks your downfall. It would help me in my capacity as High Priest if you were prepared to discuss this with me in greater detail."

"It is the least I can do, after the deaths of two of your people that have already resulted from my visit." Gesturing to the seat beside him with his bony fingers, he said, "Come and sit by me, and tell me what you wish to know."

"Do you have many gods in your world?" Nebemakhet asked.

"I am one of a family of gods, and so is Set. We each have a responsibility for one of the forces that sustain life. My father, Osiris, is God of Death and Reincarnation, and my mother, Isis, is Goddess of Love, Beauty and Fertility."

72

The High Priest had no difficulty in perceiving these words in his head, whilst ignoring the noises coming from Neb-er-tcher's beak. He had heard the Pharaoh say how difficult it was sometimes to maintain concentration during these discussions, but he – Nebemakhet – believed he had a superior ability to converse with the gods.

"Are there still more?"

"Oh yes. My grandfather, Geb, is God of Vegetation and the Earth, and his consort, Nut, is Goddess of the Sky and Resurrection. You will already know that the Supreme God is Ra, who is immortal, and he oversees all the appointments. There are other deities, but it would be tedious to go through the whole list with you now."

"And you are God of the Universe."

"Indeed I am, and my responsibility is to maintain my own world's place in the cosmos, and to reach out to other civilisations. That is why I made contact with your Pharaoh. If my pioneering visit is successful, it will open the way for the other gods to visit your land, and for your citizens to call out to them for help in times of need. "

Nebemakhet believed he now had a good understanding of what had led up to the present situation. But it did not make him feel happy to hear that all this divine assistance might one day become available. This would undermine his own status in Egypt, for he was the person people consulted if they needed any intervention from the gods. Was he not the one who had resolved the drought crisis by appeasing Khumn, the God of the Nile?

Keeping these thoughts to himself, he was impatient to learn even more – the greater his knowledge, then the more powerful it would make him. "Can you tell me something about this rival of yours, Set?"

"When he was appointed to the role of God of Darkness, he was not satisfied with this. Instead he wanted the position that was given to me. Because his protestations went unheeded, he became vengeful and evil, intent on destroying me and usurping my commission."

"In a civilisation as advanced as yours, I am surprised that you have not overcome evil," Nebemakhet commented.

Neb-er-tcher turned his gaze from the river bank and directed it toward the questioner, his brown eyes reflecting back the scene before him. "Although, as you surmise, my world is in many ways more advanced than yours, we are not all peaceful and virtuous. Crime, ambition, jealousy and other types of wickedness are still present, even if uncommon."

"But do you not have laws, and people to enforce them in your land. Also, punishment for those who transgress them?"

"Indeed, we do have systems for dealing with antisocial behaviour, but we cannot control everything that our people do. Even if we were able to do this, it would take away our individual freedom to make decisions and take actions. What might benefit one person may hinder another. Being free carries the responsibility to use that freedom wisely. Inevitably, there will be some who turn to evil and think only of themselves. Sadly, my uncle has adopted that pathway."

Nebemakhet was pleased that he had learned so much during this short encounter, but did not wish to push this relationship too quickly. "Thank you, I now understand much more about your situation and your world. I shall leave you to continue your vigil whilst I attend to my other duties, but perhaps we can talk some more at a later time."

"Of course," the God replied. "If we can all work together with a common understanding, then we shall increase our chances of a successful outcome to my visit to your world."

The High Priest returned to his cabin to think about what he had learned, and how best to use it to his own advantage. Was Neb-er-tcher being completely honest about Set? So far they had only heard one side of the story, but the true version may be different. His uncle had clearly been first in line to be appointed God of the Universe, but perhaps there was some family conflict that had resulted in a move to discredit him and give this role to his nephew. Maybe Set was only struggling to inherit the position that was rightfully his.

Nebemakhet had ambitions of his own. If he could make contact with this unfortunate rival who was forced to accept the undesirable role of God of Darkness, then perhaps there could be something to gain for both of them. But how to do this safely, and without anyone else being aware of it?

An idea came to him. These beings from another world can project their thoughts. They need transmitters to converse over long distances, and to transport themselves bodily, but would it be possible to bring about a meeting of minds, here on earth? He knew that Set was shadowing them and would not be far away. If he faced the river bank, concentrated hard and repeated Set's name, could his thoughts be read by the alien? There was only one way of finding out.

Set had found it easy to follow the progress of the boat by continuing his routine of hiding by day and travelling by night. When he needed food, he either caught it from the Nile or stole it from barns and outhouses during his nocturnal journeys. It was a week into the voyage when, as he was resting, he became aware of a voice in his head.

The phrase was being repeated over and over again: "Set, God of Darkness, I send you greetings. This is High Priest Nebemakhet on the royal barge. I wish to talk with you." His first reaction was to be suspicious, as he knew that Neb-er-tcher was also on board, and that he would be expecting an attack. If he responded to the invitation, he would be confirming that he was in the vicinity; if he ignored it, he may be wasting an opportunity to gain an accomplice.

Confident that he was clever enough to evade capture should the soldiers try to find him, he decided to risk acknowledging the message. "I hear you, High Priest, and return your greetings. What do you wish to say to me?"

When Nebemakhet heard this, he found it hard to contain his delight. At last, he was in control of a situation instead of just carrying out the bidding of the Pharaoh. One day people would realise his true worth, and wish they had acknowledged this at the time, but it would then be too late. However, he must proceed with caution to avoid being overheard, as he found it difficult to project his thoughts without audibly mouthing the words. He carefully considered what to say to the god.

"I have been talking with Neb-er-tcher," he began. "He told me that he was appointed God of the Universe when you were the rightful heir. I believe you have been treated unfairly. Perhaps I can help you remedy this shameful act so that you can accede to the position to which you are entitled."

Whilst Set was pleased to hear this, his reservation that it might not be a genuine offer remained with him. It was rare for people to perform favours without expecting something in return. Was he being lured into a trap? He needed to be sure of the motivation of this High Priest before he agreed to anything. "It is good of you to see things from my standpoint, because many are not prepared to do this. Have you discussed this with anyone else on board?" he asked.

"No, I have not," Nebemakhet replied. He chose words that he anticipated would sound convincing, rather than convey the truth. "The others are not capable of formulating their own verdict, but have just accepted without question everything that Neb-er-tcher has told them. I have reviewed the events from both sides, and my conclusion is that you should have been appointed God of the Universe."

Set paused to consider what he had heard, and decided to directly question the High Priest's motive for offering to help him. "What reward do you seek for offering to assist me?"

It was now Nebemakhet's turn to consider carefully before responding. The true reason was his lust for power, but he could not just bluntly say this. However, if his plan was successful, he would no longer have a role to play in the Pharaoh's kingdom. In fact, he would be fortunate to escape execution for treason. Could he trust Set not to just cast him aside when he had won the contest? His answer must match the question in its directness.

"God of Darkness, my position as High Priest requires me to uphold justice, correct wrongs, and reward the faithful. If I do help you I shall be branded a traitor, and my life on this earth will be finished. My hope is that you would take me back with you to your universe so that I can sit at your right hand, and be among the gods. Is this too much to ask?"

It was easy for Set to agree to this, even if he had little intention of carrying it out if and when the time came. This High Priest was ambitious, but he was prepared to betray those he worked with for personal gain. It could be just the same if he were taken to the other world. But he could be very useful now. "Yes, I could take you back to the land from where I came, and appoint you as my senior advisor. Perhaps eventually you might become a god yourself."

Nebemakhet found it difficult to contain his excitement at such a prospect, but he made an effort to do so with his reply. "Thank you, Sir; that would a great honour. But now we must think about how you can triumph over your rival, your nephew Neb-er-tcher. I shall review the situation on the barges, and talk with you again when I can suggest a plan."

"Very well," Set responded. "I shall never be far away from you, even though you will not see me. When you are ready with a proposal, just project your thoughts to the river bank like you are doing now, and I shall hear you."

The High Priest needed time to settle down. Thoughts and emotions were spinning around in his head, and he could hardly believe the successful outcome of his attempt to make contact with the God of Darkness. His colleagues may take him for granted, but one day they would have to acknowledge his superior ability and bow down before him. He did not want to risk rushing into a plan that was ill-conceived; he would take his time to watch and listen, and await an ideal opportunity.

Another week went by, and the voyage continued without incident. Then Captain Meru asked permission to board the royal barge and seek an audience with the Pharaoh. "Your Majesty, food supplies are becoming low. Up to now we have just sent a small boat to the shore to buy essential supplies from the villagers, but we need to restock the galleys. My men are starting to grumble about having to exist on dry bread and any fish they are lucky enough to catch from the Nile."

"Very well," Djoser replied. "The variety of food is also becoming limited on my vessel, and I do not wish to let our guest see us as inhospitable. When we pass the next sizeable village, steer your barge to the river bank and stock it with as much fresh produce as it will hold. Be as quick as you can, and stay alert for danger. We have not seen any sign of the Evil One, but he cannot be far away. My vessel will be safe in mid-river for the short time you are on shore."

When word of this reached Nebemakhet, he immediately realised that it could be the opportunity he had been hoping for. The royal barge would have only limited protection, and the one containing the soldiers would be vulnerable when it moored to take on supplies. He must notify Set as soon as it was safe to do so. Retiring to his cabin after the evening meal, he covered his head with a blanket and spoke as softly as he could.

"God of Darkness, this is Nebemakhet on the royal barge. Can you hear my voice?" There was no immediate response, so he repeated the message every few minutes. Had Set lost faith in him, with no desire to trust him by revealing his presence? Perhaps he had gone away, or was out of range of the voice transmission. Was his vision of mixing with the gods and maybe even becoming one of them just a naive dream? Two hours passed.

Just as he was about to cease his efforts, a voice invaded his mind. "I hear you, High Priest. It has been several days since we last spoke. What do you wish to say to me? Do you have a plan?"

"Sir, I had nearly given up hope that you would hear me tonight; it has taken a long time for you to reply."

Set's response betrayed just a hint of irritation. "You must understand that I need to remain in hiding for as long as there is any daylight. I cannot risk making any noise by speaking with you until I am sure that everyone is back in their own houses. Now, what have you found out?"

Nebemakhet felt a little foolish that he had not waited until it was completely dark before trying to contact the god. "I shall remember this in future," he said, before revealing what he had heard about the need to re-stock the barges with food.

"You have done well to tell me this," Set replied, his words serving to strengthen the High Priest's fragile ego. "Whilst the soldiers' vessel is moored at the bank, taking on supplies, I shall swim out to your vessel and see if I can confront Neb-er-tcher. Have any of the troops been stationed on the royal barge?"

"No Sir, there is just the crew and servants on board, in addition to the Pharaoh, the god, and me."

"Excellent. Then you can expect to see me when the vessels arrive at the next village to obtain the food supplies."

The conversation ended, leaving the High Priest with mixed emotions. He was looking forward to at last meeting Set, but was he doing the right thing in helping him? Would there be fighting? Would one of the gods be killed? He would have to wait until events unfolded.

Chapter 9. Confrontation

It would be another two days before the vessels reached Abydos, a settlement located on the west bank of the Nile that was large enough to have the provisions they needed. They were now past the halfway point of their journey to Aswan, and the need for fresh food was becoming a priority. Once the barges had arrived at the village, and been safely moored in mid-river, there was only an hour's daylight remaining. If the soldiers took their boat to the shore now, it would be dark before the provisions had been purchased and loaded.

Captain Meru discussed the situation with the Pharaoh. The only trouble they had experienced had been right at the start of the voyage, when the guards had not been vigilant. Now that security had been strengthened, and nothing more had been seen or heard from Set, the two men felt confident that it would be safe to take on the much-needed food without delay. Thus, the order was given for the accompanying barge to raise anchor and row to the jetty next to the village, leaving the royal vessel with its few passengers alone and unprotected.

Nebemakhet wondered if he should try to contact his new-found associate to apprise him of the current situation, but decided that he might be overheard. He need not have concerned himself. Once Set knew of the intention to leave the barge with his adversary on board without any guards, he had doubled his nocturnal travel distance to find the next sizeable village along the river. He had arrived at Abydos before the boats and, a short time later, was watching from his hiding place as they sailed into view.

As the soldiers moored their vessel at the landing stage and went about their business, spurred on by thoughts of the fresh food they would be enjoying that evening, the God of Darkness seized his opportunity. Despite the twilight not affording him the invisibility he would have preferred, he entered the river and swam toward the royal barge. Staying underwater as much as possible, his eyes protected by their nictitating membranes, he reached the vessel without being seen.

The members of the royal party were walking up and down on deck, wishing they could be taking a stroll on shore but realising that it would be too dangerous. Set waited until Neb-er-tcher was opposite him, then quickly launched himself upwards, grabbed him by the throat, and pulled him over the side of the boat. Nebemakhet only had a brief view of the Evil One, but was shocked to see how different he looked to the God of the Universe.

The High Priest and the Pharaoh rushed to the handrail and peered down into the
inky water. There was no sign of either of the aliens. "Go quickly and fetch the lantern," Djoser barked. "The daylight has almost gone, and we shall have difficulty seeing anything without it." Left alone on deck, he tried to attract the attention of the soldiers on shore, but his shouting went unheard.

"I have brought some of the servants to help us search," the High Priest said when returned, breathing heavily from his exertion. The men spread out along the handrail and looked down at the river, searching for anything that might indicate that the gods were there.

One of the servants shouted excitedly: "Your Majesty, I think I can see a stain in the water that might be blood."

"Take off your white apron and dip it into the water at that spot," the Pharaoh said. Pointing to one of the oars stowed on the deck, he added, "Here, tie it to this if you need to reach out." The man carried out the instruction, and they all inspected the white cloth.

"There is some redness there," the High Priest observed. "But it has been diluted so much that we cannot be certain just what it is."

"We must attract the soldiers on the bank to come and search," Djoser said. They all shouted and waved. Eventually they were seen. Captain Meru looked toward the royal barge but the darkness prevented him seeing anything except the lantern and some shadowy figures. But they were shouting something he could not quite hear. Realising that there must be something wrong, he needed to return to the vessel as quickly as possible to see if they needed help.

He called the soldiers together. "We must stop loading the food, and go back to the other boat as quickly as possible. The Pharaoh and his party appear to be in difficulty." This order was not well received by the men, who were savouring the reward of a special dinner for their efforts, but it was not for them to question it. Reluctantly, they climbed aboard and set course for the mid-river rendezvous.

As soon as they were alongside the royal barge Djoser quickly explained what had happened. He then said to Meru: "You must row around the barge and then continue in ever-widening circles, searching the water for anything that might indicate what happened to the aliens. Go now."

They were only on their second circuit when one of the soldiers shouted: "Captain Meru, there looks to be a body floating out there to the right." They rowed toward it. It was Neb-er-tcher; he was alive but bleeding from a deep gash on his shoulder. The men carefully pulled him on board and headed back toward the Pharaoh's barge.

"We have found the God of the Universe," Meru shouted. "He is not dead, but badly wounded. We shall be back with you in a minute or two."

"Is there any sign of Set, the Evil One?" Djoser shouted back.

"No Sir, we have not seen him, but we shall continue looking." They transferred their guest to the royal boat and then cast off to continue the search, their weapons at the ready.

Neb-er-tcher was weak through loss of blood, but remained conscious. The priority was to clean and bandage his wound. Once this was done, the Pharaoh said, "I sincerely regret that this has occurred whilst you are a guest on my barge, and under the protection of my men."

"Do not take the blame upon yourself," the God replied. "Set would have found a way to attack me somewhere, sometime, whatever I was doing." After a pause to gain some strength, he continued, "But it does seem a coincidence that he seemed to know that I would be on an unguarded boat today, and in the failing light. Was he just lucky, or did he know beforehand this would be the case?"

"I cannot think who might have informed him," Djoser said. "He must have been carefully observing our movements and just seized the opportunity when it presented itself."

Nebemakhet was feeling very uncomfortable, and just hoped that this was not obvious to the others. He was glad when the Pharaoh changed the subject and asked the god, "How serious is your injury? Are you going to recover?"

"I shall eventually be fully recovered," Neb-er-tcher replied. "I informed you earlier that those who inhabit my world are able to regenerate some parts of the body when they are lost or injured. In time, my wound will heal."

There was another question that everyone wanted to ask, and the High Priest had more reason to do so than had the others. "Can you tell us what happened after you were pulled into the water?"

"Yes. Set immediately tried to stab me in the neck with his sharp beak, just as he did with the unfortunate guard at the pyramid. But I managed to move sideways and instead he caught me on the top of my shoulder. I placed both my hands around his thin neck, and squeezed. Then I held him under the water. We were both fighting for breath, and I was on the verge of releasing him, desperate to go up for some air. But Set's body then became limp and I let him go. He sank beneath me, and I was then able to reach the surface."

"Is the God of Darkness now dead?" Nebemakhet tried to make this sound like an innocent question, but the implications for him were many now that he had committed himself to working with the one whom everybody else regarded as evil.

"I do not know, and you can never make assumptions. Perhaps we shall not see him again, but maybe we shall. We must remain alert at all times, and not leave ourselves in the same vulnerable state as we were on this occasion. If he lives, he will certainly strike again, and he is ruthless enough to kill anybody who gets in his way."

"Should we continue searching for Set's body?" Djoser asked.

"I think this would be futile now," Neb-er-tcher replied. "If he is dead, he will be at the bottom of the river and the current will have taken him downstream. If he is alive, he will know how to avoid being seen."

"Very well, I shall call to Captain Meru to abandon the search. The soldiers might as well enjoy some of the food they managed to take on board before they had to leave Abydos so quickly."

A short time later, a shadowy figure waded unsteadily from the water and onto the uninhabited east bank of the river, to seek out a place to hide.

Next morning the boats resumed their journey. Having already had two encounters with the God of Darkness on this voyage, with one resulting in a fatality, the party was determined to avoid another. Guards were posted on the royal barge, and it would not be left on its own in the river again. Although food stocks were not as great as they should have been, due to having to abort the restocking at Abydos, they would suffice for the remainder of the voyage if they were careful.

Nebemakhet tried to limit meeting with the other members of the royal party, in case he inadvertently gave hints of his involvement in the latest attack. The shock of Set's appearance, glimpsed only briefly, had not left him, for he had not anticipated it would be so different from that of their guest. He spent as much time as possible alone in his cabin, listening for a message from his new associate that would indicate he was still alive. Several days passed, but he heard nothing.

Perhaps Set was dead, strangled by Neb-er-tcher. Was his dream of being elevated to the status of a god ended before it had even begun? He needed to know what lay ahead, and decided to take the initiative and try to make contact with the Evil One. That evening, when he was sure he would not be overheard, he faced the river bank, concentrated hard and said: "Set, God of Darkness, this is High Priest Nebemakhet. Are you alive? Do you hear my voice?"

He waited, but there was no response. He repeated the words. Still nothing came back to him. His left leg was starting to develop cramp, so he changed his position and faced in the opposite direction. Once again he tried to project his message. He was about to abort his attempts before he was discovered by others on the barge, when he heard a voice in his head. "I can hear you, High Priest. Yes, I am alive."

Nebemakhet was overjoyed, and had difficulty keeping his voice low. "I feared you might be lying dead at the bottom of the river. Have you been injured?"

"We do not die quite so easily," Set replied. "I deliberately went limp when Neb-er-tcher held me under the water, so that he would let me go. He was already injured and his strength was weakened. It was easy for me to make my way to the east bank once I was free of him. Tell me, is he seriously hurt?"

"No, Sir, unfortunately he is not. He was quickly taken from the river and his wound bandaged. He says it will heal quickly. But what now? The security on the barges has been increased, and it will be difficult for you to make any further attempts on Neb-er-tcher's life."

"I can see that for myself. You are now only two days from your destination at Aswan, and I shall wait for you on Elephantine Island. If you want the reward you crave for, you must then help me to confront my nephew when he is not surrounded by the guards."

Nebemakhet was starting to feel very uncomfortable again, but he tried not to reveal this in his response. "Very well, God of Darkness, I shall assess the situation once we have arrived. We should end our conversation now, before I am overheard and our secret pact exposed."

Whilst the High Priest was pleased that Set was still alive, and determined to succeed with his plan to defeat Neb-er-tcher, his satisfaction was tempered by concerns that he would again be expected to help. He was not one who obtained any pleasure from seeing somebody die, let alone be a party to it. Perhaps his ambition had overridden his ability to think clearly and act rationally. Would he regret this some day? But if he withdrew his support for Set now, he might become the next victim. No, he was caught up in this situation and must remain with it to the end.

Despite taking care to avoid being overheard during the conversation he had just

had with Set, he had not been completely successful. Neb-er-tcher had been walking around the barge, using the exercise to help him return to full fitness. His sharp hearing had detected faint noises coming from the High Priest's cabin. Curious to know what was going on when he knew that the occupant would be alone, he had stopped and listened.

He would not normally have tried to eaves-drop on another's conversation but the recent attempt on his life, and the unanswered questions it posed, had made him alert to anything unusual that was happening. His ability to mentally both project and receive messages enabled him to grasp the essence of what was being said on the other side of the door.

Set had obviously not perished after the two of them had grappled in the river. What he then heard confirmed his suspicion that somebody had been informing on him. For the Evil One to know when to attack, he must have had some prior knowledge of the plan to take on supplies of food. The informant had now been identified, but Neb-er-tcher decided to keep this information to himself, at least for the present. It would be useful to monitor future conversations so that he could be ready for any further attempt on his life.

The last stage of the voyage was uneventful. As evening approached, the two barges anchored in mid-river off the southern end of Elephantine Island. The Pharaoh asked Captain Meru to join the others on the royal barge to discuss how they would handle the shore excursion. Once they had left the relative safety of the vessels and disembarked onto the island, they would be more vulnerable to attack.

Djoser began: "I must remind you that the reason we are here at Aswan is to give our guest, the God of the Universe, the opportunity to help us avoid the droughts that occur when the river does not flood. The temple dedicated to Khumn, the God of the Nile is on Elephantine Island, and we shall need to visit it, just as Nebemakhet did many years ago."

The mention of his name made the High Priest feel important, and he believed it was appropriate for him to comment. "Yes, I visited the temple and so did Captain Meru. I took the decision to carry out what renovations were possible with the resources at our disposal. Then, I instructed that tithes must be regularly left for the god. Khumn must be pleased because the river has flooded every year since my intervention."

"Yes indeed, we are grateful for your actions," the Pharaoh commented, before quickly returning to his more immediate concern. "If Set is still alive, my question is, how are we going to guarantee the safety of our guest, as well as ourselves, from another attack that next time might result in the loss of more lives?"

"We have nineteen troops left at our disposal," Captain Meru said. "If all are there to guard you on the island, we should be safe, but then Set could come and sabotage the barges, perhaps killing the servants who remained on board."

It was a bizarre situation. Two people there knew that the God of Darkness was alive, but neither would disclose it at this point in time. One of them would be happy if the landing party were attacked and Neb-er-tcher defeated. The other wished to know when and where such a confrontation would take place, so that he could prepare himself for it.

It was Nebemakhet who decided to speak up and try to manipulation the arrangements. "I agree that we should not risk losing the boats or its crew, therefore I suggest that half the soldiers stay and guard the vessels whilst the remainder accompany the landing party. Nine or ten men should be more than a match for Set, assuming of course that he is still alive."

Nobody offered an alternative plan. "Very well," the Pharaoh said, "we shall remain in mid-river tonight, and double the guards on lookout. Tomorrow morning both the barges will proceed to the shore and moor as near to the temple site as possible. The landing party, and half of the soldiers, will then disembark and carry out its mission as quickly as it is possible to do so. Any questions?"

There were no questions. "Very well," Djoser concluded, "I suggest we obtain some rest and prepare ourselves for tomorrow's expedition."

Chapter 10. Elephantine Island

Back in his cabin, Nebemakhet needed some time to decide whether or not to try and make contact with Set again. The God of Darkness was almost certainly already observing the boats, and knew that some of the party would be making a visit to the temple. But he did not know exactly when this would be, and how many guards would be present. The High Priest still wanted to show that he was helping the Evil One with his plan, so it was difficult to resist telling him what he knew.

Reclining on his bed, again with a blanket over his head, he wondered which way to face. Was Set already on the island? He correctly assumed this was the case, and began: "God of Darkness, I have something to say to you. Can you hear my voice?"

After repeating this several times, the reply came back: "I can hear you, High Priest. Do you have something useful to tell me?"

Ignoring what he regarded as a hint of sarcasm, Nebemakhet replied, "Tomorrow morning the barges will moor alongside the island. The royal party, accompanied by no more than ten of the soldiers, will disembark and make an expedition to Khumn's temple. I shall be among them."

"Where will the rest of the troops be?"

Here was a chance to boast. "At my suggestion, they will remain on the vessels and guard them until the landing party returns. This will mean that your rival will have less protection than might otherwise have been the case."

Set was shrewd enough to know the game that his informant was playing, but it would be useful to keep him happy, at least whilst he was needed. "You have done well," he said. "I shall consider what to do, but if you can manage to separate Neb-er-tcher from the others whilst you are on the island, if only for a moment, it will give me the chance to strike him."

The thought of helping a murderer commit his evil act, and perhaps seeing a blood-stained body fall at his feet, once again caused the High Priest to feel discomfort. His calling identified him as a man of peace, but his burning ambition to be among the gods themselves overrode any consideration of what was morally right or wrong. "I shall try to do so if the opportunity presents itself," he eventually replied.

"Then let us end this conversation now, and prepare ourselves for the events of tomorrow," were Set's final words.

Neb-er-tcher had no need to try to eavesdrop on any discussion the High Priest

may have had with the Evil One, because he was sure that his adversary was already close by, and would try to stage an attack the following day. He would be ready for it this time, and be alert for any sign that he was being lured into a trap. There had been many fights between them in their younger days, but neither of them had ever emerged as a clear victor.

As dawn broke next morning the sky was streaked with red. When Nebemakhet awoke after a troubled night and saw this, he wondered if this was an omen that blood would be spilled that day. It did little to calm the turmoil within him, and he just hoped that this would not be obvious when he joined the rest of the landing party.

As the barges tied up alongside Elephant Island and the passengers assembled on the shore, Captain Meru broke off from assembling the troops that would be accompanying them and approached Neb-er-tcher. "Sir, we know there might be an attempt on your life whilst we are here." Offering him a sword he said, "I suggest you wear this on your belt so that you will be able to defend yourself."

"That is very considerate of you," the God replied, "but in my land we do not use weapons like this. We have learned to avoid violence but, when it does occur, our evolution has left us with sharp beaks, fingers that can become claws, and feet that can kick strongly. If we need to fight, we use what nature has given us. You have already seen the injuries that Set has been able to inflict."

"I am impressed, and admire you for this," Meru said. "We would be a better species on this earth if we were able to throw away our weapons of war. My only concern is that a skilful leader could be physically weak. Without weapons to defend himself, he could easily be overthrown."

"Perhaps your own evolution will eventually eliminate the need for such weaponry. But whilst I decline your invitation to carry a sword, what I do request is a stick to help me with the walk to the temple. Some of the effects of the recent attack on me remain. If there is no well-trodden path to follow, and we have to push our way through the undergrowth, I do not wish to stumble or trap the claws on my feet in the gaps between the stones."

This request was easily fulfilled, and a few minutes later a sturdy walking stick had been fashioned from the branch of a tree. Neb-er-tcher accepted this gratefully – it might have more uses than just being a walking aid.

The group set off for the temple. Captain Meru led the way, as he was familiar with the geography after having worked at Aswan for so long when the pyramid stones were being cut. Four soldiers followed, and then the three members of the royal party, with the remaining five men taking up the rear. They proceeded carefully, ever watchful of a surprise attack from the evil Set. Eventually the temple came into view, and the posse emerged from the trees and into the clearing. They had arrived without incident, but were now a long way from the relative safety of the barges, and out of hailing distance of the additional troops that were waiting there.

Whilst they were taking a short break before entering the building, Nebemakhet took the opportunity to try and influence the thinking of those around him. He said to the God of the Universe, but in a voice that others could hear: "Perhaps we are being too cautious, worrying about an attack from Set. We have seen no trace of the Evil One since you did battle with him in the river. It is most likely that he is lying dead at the bottom of the Nile at this moment."

Neb-er-tcher was fully aware of the High Priest's game, but was happy to play along with it, at least for the present. "You may be correct, and we certainly are taking many precautions. But we must not make any assumptions. My uncle may be dead, or injured; he may be many kilometres away, or close by. Let us not relax our vigilance too much. Come, let us go and have a look inside the temple."

A pair of small, black eyes peered out from the undergrowth, and watched them enter.

Once again the High Priest lost no time in again boasting about his achievements. "When I came here the first time, the temple had been neglected. It was an insult to the God of the Nile, and I immediately ordered cleaning and renovations to take place. Once the building was in good order, I gave instructions that tithes of food must be regularly offered to Khumn. I then prayed earnestly that the flooding of the river would recommence. My prayers were answered – later that year the floods came."

During this monologue, no mention was made of Meru and his contribution to the mission. The Captain had readily supplied the labour from among his stone masons at the Aswan quarry, supervised the renovations, and arranged for the tithes to be brought to the temple. For as long as he remained at Aswan, he had made personal visits to check that all was well.

The Pharaoh had said little since the party had stepped onto the island. This was his first visit here, and he had been content to listen what the others were saying, whilst keeping a watchful eye open for any sign of danger. He now considered it was an appropriate time to reassert his authority. "Yes, we are grateful for what you achieved here on your previous mission, Nebemakhet, and for the help given by Captain Meru." The High Priest forced a pained smile at the acknowledgement that he had not acted alone.

Turning his attention to their guest, he continued, "God of the Universe, we are now in the sanctuary of Khumn, who controls the river. We came here because you said you had an idea that might ensure the flood occurs each year without fail. You now have the opportunity to intervene with the god of the Nile in his own house."

"Very well. I ask you all to move away from the altar and remain quiet so that I can try to join my mind with that of Khumn." The onlookers saw Neb-er-tcher close his eyes. His hawk-like beak was moving, but no sound could be heard coming from it. The minutes passed very slowly for the party, and they wondered if their guest had gone to sleep. Should they approach and try to rouse him?

He then suddenly opened his eyes and exclaimed: "It is just as I suspected. Khumn is not one of the gods from my own universe. Indeed, he is not a god from any universe. He was just a priest who sacrificed himself to the Nile many years ago, in an attempt to make the river flood. Later in that same year it did resume its life-giving deluge. The citizens attributed this to the martyrdom of their holy man, and elevated him to the status of a god. This temple is dedicated to his memory."

This came as unexpected news, and there was a period of silence whilst the implications of the revelation were realised. "Is this individual still someone who can be prayed to for help?" Nebemakhet asked, in an attempt to preserve his reputation. It was starting to look like all the credit he was claiming for the resumption of the Nile flooding might be taken away from him.

"No, he will not hear your pleas, just as he did not hear mine when I called to him a few minutes ago. The information I obtained came from Tefnut, the God of Rain. When I reached out to see if there was anyone listening who had the power to detect my thoughts, it was he who answered."

The High Priest made an effort to control the sense of panic that was enveloping him, but tried to keep his voice calm. "Are you implying that the resumption of the flood was not the result of praying to Khumn, caring for his temple, and offering tithes?"

"Yes. If what Tefnut told me is true, then the work you did here did not result in the Nile flooding later in the year." Realising that these words may be disappointing to some of the party, he added by way of consolation: "But it was good to restore this fine building, and help to preserve the memory of the one who died in the belief that it would bring an end to the drought."

Whilst Nebemakhet remained silent and tried to conceal his deflated ego, Captain Meru spoke up. "I agree that it was right to maintain this memorial to the courageous Khumn, and I was happy to give my assistance to the High Priest when he asked for it. But, if this did not cause the flood to resume, then what did?"

"Tefnut said that the deluge does not occur at the whim of any god, but is the result of heavy rain occurring many kilometres south of here, combined with snow melting on the distant mountains. If the amount of rain and snow that falls is low, then little water is added to the river and there is no flood."

The Pharaoh had been carefully taking note of all that was being said, and now asked the obvious question. "Thanks to you, God of the Universe, we now know much more about the behaviour of the river. But, when the droughts occur, they cause much hardship in our land. If we cannot influence when it will overflow and irrigate the fields, what are we to do? Should we now direct our prayers to this new god, Tefnut, and ask him to send the rain?"

Neb-er-tcher's beak was unable to smile, and the chirping noises coming from it could not convey emotion in the way that a human voice can. "Is this the way you address all your difficulties – praying to the relevant god and asking him or her to favour your requests? Had you not thought that what pleases you may cause hardship for others? If the rains are heavy in the lands to the south, people may lose their homes, their animals, and perhaps even their lives. Do you believe you are more important than these folk?"

Djoser was surprised at this barbed response, but he tried to retain an air of calmness and dignity. "I did not mean to imply this but, when we were first in communication with each other, you said that your mission in coming to Egypt was to help us to become a great nation. What, then, can you suggest we do to help avoid the devastating droughts that descend on us every few years?"

"The answer lies in conserving during times of plenty, and using what is stored when there is a shortage. This is just what you do already with your food."

97

"Do continue," Djoser urged, nodding in agreement. "We are listening."

"You must build many dams and reservoirs along the banks of the Nile where your farmers live and work. When the river floods, trap as much water as you can, and not just what you need for one season. Then, in the years when there is no deluge, the stored water can be used for the crops and animals."

"This is indeed a useful suggestion, and some of our farmers are already doing what you say, but only in a small way. When we return to Memphis, I shall meet with Imhotep and ask him to design suitable storage facilities."

Neb-er-tcher continued: "There is something else that you can do, but it will be a much larger undertaking. If you build a dam here at Aswan, you will be able to hold back some of the water during the floods, and release it when the flow of the river is low."

"This would certainly be very effective," the Pharaoh replied. "But it will require a great deal of resources to span the river like you have suggested. I shall also discuss this with the Vizier when I meet with him. If we cannot manage to do this ourselves, I am sure that some time in the future such a dam will be built." Looking around at the others gathered in the sanctuary, he added: "Is there anything else we should do whilst we are on the island?"

It was Captain Meru who responded first. "Your Majesty, we are exposed to danger for as long as we remain here. We have seen nothing of Set, and do not know if he is still alive, but the risk of attack remains. I suggest we return to the relative safety of the barges. We can continue this discussion as we walk."

Nobody spoke out against this, so the group arranged itself in the same order as it was on the outward trek, and started to make its way back to the landing site.

Again a pair of eyes watched them as they left the temple. Set's ability to communicate mentally had enabled him to intercept

Neb-er-tcher's broadcast to any deity who could hear him. He had also heard Tefnut's response. Once the party was out of sight, he discretely followed them, hoping that the High Priest would create an opportunity for him to attack his nephew.

Nebemakhet was making a great effort to remain calm, and give the impression he was not upset by the revelation that his work at the temple all those years ago was not responsible for the resumption of the flooding. He made sure he was next to Neb-er-tcher as they wended their way through the trees. Whilst previously his feelings toward the God of the Universe may have been neutral, now he hated him for destroying his reputation as the man who had ended the drought.

The soldiers were weary. Most of them had been up during the night, taking their turns at guard duty. Their main motivation now was to return to the barges, have something to eat, and then rest. So far there had been no sign of the Evil One, and vigilance was not as sharp as it should have been.

The High Priest let one of the rearguard troops overtake them, and then another. The remaining three lagged behind. When they were out of sight around a bend in the path, he seized the opportunity to carry out his plan.

"When we were walking towards the temple earlier today, I thought I noticed an inscribed stone in the bushes," Nebemakhet said to his companion. "It may be at about this spot. Can I show it to you? You might be able to decipher the inscription."

Neb-er-tcher took a firm grip on his walking stick, and left the path to go where the High Priest was pointing. This was just what Set had been waiting for, and he seized his opportunity. Rushing forward he stretched out his arms to grab hold of his adversary, but the God of the Universe was ready for him. Raising his walking stick, he pointed it forward and the Evil One ran straight into it. The tip caught him in the middle of the chest; there was a cracking sound, indicating that ribs had been broken.

Uttering a screech of pain, Set sank to the ground. Neb-er-tcher tried to hit him over the head with the stick to knock him unconscious but his opponent, though injured, was too quick for him. He jerked his head to one side, grabbed the stick, and pulled his nephew down.

The two of them grappled, with the Evil One repeatedly trying to penetrate Neb-er-tcher's neck with his sharp beak. As he did when they fought in the river, the God of the Universe gripped Set by the throat and squeezed as tightly as he could, oblivious of the blood leaking from the fresh wounds on his shoulder and arm. Eventually the Evil One's body became limp. With an effort, Neb-er-tcher started to raise himself, but his loss of blood caused him to quickly collapse and lie motionless on the ground.

Nebemakhet had been content to stand back and take no part in this confrontation, but it now seemed that both these visiting deities had perished. The time was now right to call for help. He took the few steps back to the path and shouted as loud as he could. The soldiers came running, and the High Priest led them to where he had left the bodies. Only that of the God of the Universe remained, the blood from his wounds staining the grass that surrounded him.

Chapter 11. The investigation

The commotion quickly brought the rest of the landing party to the scene of the attack, and Captain Meru's training immediately led him to take charge of the situation. "You five," he barked, pointing to the soldiers who had been taking up the rear. "Spread out and search the vicinity for any sign of Set."

The Pharaoh's first concern was with the unconscious deity lying on the ground. "Have we lost Neb-er-tcher? Is he dead?"

Meru bent down and felt for any sign of a heart beat in the prone figure. "I am not familiar with the anatomy of his species, but I think I can detect a pulse. He is still alive but very weak." Raising his voice to address everyone he said, "We must bind his wounds quickly. Tear strips of cloth from your clothing so that I can use them as bandages. Quickly! Do it now!"

Whilst the Captain was doing his best to staunch the flow of blood, Djoser approached the High Priest and asked in an authoritative voice, "Nebemakhet, tell us what happened. You were with our guest; why did you leave the path?"

Nebemakhet knew that he could be in serious trouble, so he resorted to lying. Neb-er-tcher might not live to recount his version but, if he did, hopefully he would not remember the precise details. "Your Majesty, we were walking along behind you when my companion pointed toward what he thought might be an inscribed stone, party hidden in the undergrowth. Before I could stop him, he dashed into the bushes to investigate. I quickly followed."

"What happened next? How was he attacked?"

"Just as I caught up with him, the Evil One leapt out from behind a tree. They both fell to the ground, fighting. I tried to intervene but was not able to separate them, so I shouted for help."

"And where were the soldiers whilst all this was happening?"

"Sir, I don't know. Perhaps they did not see us suddenly leave the path, and just assumed that we were still ahead of them."

"Once we are back in the safety of the barges, Captain Meru will conduct an investigation," the Pharaoh said. "Disciplinary action must be taken against his negligent troops, as this is the second time they have failed to prevent our guest from being attacked."

Their first priority was to take the wounded Neb-er-tcher back to the boats, where he could receive more careful attention. They needed something on which they could carry him. "You men," Meru said, pointing to two of his soldiers. "Run back to the temple and see if you can find something flat that we can use as a stretcher. Go quickly!"

The soldiers soon returned with the top of a wooden table that had been used to prepare food for the altar. The injured alien was carefully lifted on to it, and the party made its way back toward the river. They all kept close together, ready for any further attack that might be made. Few words were spoken, but each person had thoughts that eventually would have to be expressed.

Nebemakhet was not sure if his claim of innocence would survive, once the others had had the time to review the situation in more detail. The God of the Universe was obviously seriously wounded but, if he survived, would he tell a different story and expose the lies that he had told in order to protect himself? Then there was the matter of Set. Yes, he was able to remove himself from the site of the attack, but what was the extent of his injuries? Should he try to make contact with him, or wait to see if he received a message?

The Pharaoh was both angry and embarrassed that his guest had suffered a second attack whilst under his care. There was something puzzling about this latest attempt. There they all were, keeping close together, alert to the possibility of the Evil One making another attempt to overpower Neb-er-tcher. But he and the High Priest deliberately left the safety of the rest of the party and went into the bushes. He had already heard one version of the event. If the alien did not die, questions needed to be asked of him.

Captain Meru also had some serious interrogating to do, once they had all reached the safety of the barges. The troops were there to guard the others, so how did two members of the party manage to leave the path unseen? Either the men were seriously negligent, or they had been tricked. The security of the expedition rested on his shoulders, and he had let everyone down yet again. He was a professional soldier, proud of his achievements – until now. Would his military career be at an end?

They reached the vessels without further incident, and carefully lifted Neb-er-tcher onto the royal barge. Meru ensured that their patient was made as comfortable as possible, and then sought out more suitable dressings to bind his wounds. "He is still alive, but very weak," he said, in answer to the Pharaoh's anxious question. "Thankfully, the bandages have stemmed the bleeding, but he has lost a lot of fluid. We must try to force some liquid down his throat."

Whilst the god was receiving the best nursing possible with the limited means available on board, the vessels were manoeuvred into mid-river to begin their long journey home. Djoser decided that the enquiry into what happened on the island could wait until morning. The main need now was for some food and rest. Meru ordered two of the soldiers to take turns in maintaining a bed-side vigil of their patient, both to guard him and to immediately report any deterioration in his condition. There must be no more mistakes!

The Pharaoh arose as soon as it was light. He immediately went into Neb-er-tcher's cabin, and was very relieved to see that his eyes were open and his beak was emitting some faint musical chirps. "Sir," said the soldier, "He has been making these noises for over an hour, but I can't understand what he is saying."

"Very well," Djoser responded. "You may go now and join your colleagues. I shall stay here with him." When the soldier had departed, he moved close to his guest and said: "I deeply regret what happened to you. How are you feeling now?"

It was difficult to interpret the weak sounds, but the Pharaoh had had more experience than anyone else in communicating with the alien. "Do not trouble yourself, I shall recover," Neb-er-tcher said. "I told you that we have developed the ability to repair ourselves."

"That is good news. Are you able to take some food and drink?"

"Yes, thank you, I shall try to eat something – perhaps some of those dates that I like. But I do not remember how I came to be back on the barge. You must have carried me here."

"You have Captain Meru to thank for that," Djoser said. "He immediately took action to bind your wounds and bring you back on board. But we can save further discussion until you have gained some strength. Rest now, and I shall give instructions for some refreshment to be brought to you."

Whilst the barges made their slow way northwards against the prevailing winds, there was much to do on board. When he

104

considered that Neb-er-tcher was strong enough to discuss what had taken place on the island, the Pharaoh again joined him in his cabin. "Nebemakhet told me that you had seen what might have been an inscribed stone in the bushes, and left the path to investigate. Is that what happened?"

Neb-er-tcher clearly remembered the incident, but chose not to expose the High Priest's deliberate treachery at this time. It would be useful to let the communication between him and Set continue, so that he could eavesdrop on the messages. "The injuries I received must have dulled my memory, because I am uncertain of the exact sequence of events," he said untruthfully. "All I know is that we left the path together to go and look at something in the undergrowth."

"And did you find an inscribed stone or anything else of interest?"

"The attack from Set came unexpectedly. We never reached the spot where the artefact might have been."

"Did Nebemakhet try to defend you, or fight your attacker?" Djoser asked, still struggling with doubts that he was developing a full understanding of the true version of the events.

"I do not know, for I soon lost consciousness. Perhaps we have the High Priest to thank for chasing away my adversary. I knew nothing more until I woke up on this barge."

The Pharaoh did not want to cause his guest additional stress by pressing him for more details. "Very well, we can leave it at that for the present. I repeat my profound sadness that you have been attacked twice whilst being under my protection. It must not happen again. I want to find out why the troops were not guarding you all the time; if they had been, this incident would not have occurred."

Captain Meru had lost no time in conducting his own investigation with the soldiers. He lined up the nine men on deck, and made little effort to control his anger at the way they had failed to prevent the attack on their visitor. "Your specific instruction was to guard the group and prevent any attempt to attack Neb-er-tcher," he shouted. "Four of you were positioned at the front, and five at the rear, but the God and High Priest still left the path and not one of you noticed. I want an explanation!"

Silence followed, with each of the soldiers hoping that someone else would be the first to speak. Meru pointed to one of them and said, "Speak man; I want an answer."

"Captain, I was in the rear contingent and could see the two members of the royal party in front of me. They were walking very slowly. One of my companions went past them, and then another. We were looking to the right and the left to spot any sign of the Evil One, and did not notice that those whom we were guarding had disappeared."

"At least you have given me an honest answer," Meru said, only slightly calmer. "But this is inexcusable conduct from professional soldiers. Our guest is severely injured and any of us, including you men, could have been killed. If there are any further incidents whilst we are on this mission, I shall tie you all up and leave you in the desert for the God of Darkness to come and feast on you. As it is, you will all lose a day's pay. You are dismissed."

The Captain was not sure if he had heard the full story. These were trained troops, and they knew what they had to do. How could they be so negligent as to just walk straight past those whom they were entrusted to guard? Whatever the true reason, they had failed in their duty and needed to be punished. Security on this trip was his responsibility, and his own reputation as an army officer was already suffering. There had to be no more mishaps.

Nebemakhet was expecting to be sent for at any moment, once the Pharaoh had spoken with Neb-er-tcher and almost certainly been told that it was he, the High Priest, who had led their alien visitor off the path and away from the rest of the party. When the call came, he entered the Pharaoh's cabin fearing that his plan to aid Set had been exposed. The penalty for such treachery would be execution.

"I have asked our alien guest what happened on the island," Djoser began. Nebemakhet could already feel the sword against his neck.

"He can remember very little due to his injuries and loss of blood. All he can recall is that the two of you left the path to look at something in the bushes, and that the attack came quickly. He soon lost consciousness and knows nothing more until he woke up on the barge."

The High Priest tried not to show the intense relief he felt from hearing this. Perhaps he had been lucky enough to avoid blame on this occasion, but he would have to be very careful not to risk another situation for which he could be held responsible. "How is the God of the Universe now?" he asked.

"He is weak and it will take some time for him to recover his strength," the Pharaoh replied. "We have now failed to prevent two attacks on him, and there must not be another. Neb-er-tcher must be accompanied at all times during this voyage. I shall ask Captain Meru to arrange for one of the soldiers always to be close to him, but you and I must also spend as much time as we can in his presence."

"I am glad to hear that he will survive," Nebemakhet felt himself obliged to comment. "We do not want to lose our important visitor after all the effort we have made to bring him here." He was now feeling confident that he was not under any suspicion.

But his sense of relief was about to be shaken.

"There is just one thing that worries me," Djoser said. "You told me earlier that Neb-er-tcher darted into the undergrowth to look at something, before you had time to stop him."

"Yes, Your Majesty, that is indeed what happened."

"But you both knew how dangerous that would be. The soldiers were there to guard you. Did they see you leave the path?"

The High Priest knew that he had to be careful with his responses. "I looked in both directions, but did not see any of the men. My only recourse was to follow my companion to try and protect him, if it were necessary to do so."

"But you were too late to help to defend him when Set attacked?"

"It all happened so quickly. I tried to intervene but they were both on the ground. That is when I decided to call for help." Was his version of the event being doubted? Nebemakhet wondered. Had the God of the Universe said more than the Pharaoh had just reported?

"Very well," Djoser said. "I am sure you did what you thought was right, but we had planned this expedition carefully so as to avoid any risk to our alien guest. It has nearly ended in disaster on at least two occasions. We must learn from these experiences and take no further chances of any sort. If anything else goes wrong on this voyage, nobody will escape punishment."

The High Priest returned to his cabin; his heart still beating rapidly due to his narrow escape from blame. He needed time to think about his current situation. The Pharaoh was clearly unconvinced that he understood the true version of events, but was not able to contradict what he had been told. Nevertheless, the warning had been given, and he had to avoid any chance that he could be implicated in any future incident.

What had Neb-er-tcher actually revealed to Djoser about what happened? If he had given an accurate account, this would have put him under suspicion of having deliberately enticed the God away from the path. But this accusation had not been made. Either the alien had forgotten, or he was being frugal with the truth. If the latter, then why?

He wondered again if he should he try to contact Set. Was he still alive? Yes, he had been able to remove himself from the scene of the attack by the time the soldiers arrived, but he could have been mortally wounded. Maybe he should leave matters to settle down for a few days before trying to communicate with him again. Unless, that is, he was contacted first.

The voyage back to Memphis continued uneventfully. Neb-er-tcher slowly gained strength, but it would take many weeks before he was back to full fitness. As the Pharaoh had commanded, he was never left on his own. Nebemakhet tried to avoid being the one to stay with him, especially if nobody else was present. When his turn did come, he avoided raising the topic of the attack, and was relieved that the God also did not speak about it.

They were more than half way home before the High Priest heard the voice. His sleep was interrupted when his name was called. Thinking that he was being summoned to carry out some duty, he was about to rise from his bed when he realised that the words were entering directly into his head and not through his ears. "Nebemakhet, this is Set. Can you hear me?" After a pause, the question was repeated, and then again.

Once he was sure that his mind was not playing tricks on him, he replied. "Yes, God of Darkness, this is the High Priest. I am relieved to know that you are alive." He still found this form of communication difficult to carry out without mouthing the words as he tried to project them.

"Although I managed to drag myself away from the place of the attack just before the soldiers arrived, several of my ribs were cracked by the stick that Neb-er-tcher was holding. It was several days before I was able to follow the vessels, and I have only now caught up with you. I am still in pain."

"I am sorry to hear this, but you have done well to travel this far," Nebemakhet said. "Security is now very tight on board, and Neb-er-tcher is never left alone. It would be unwise to mount another assault on his life whilst we are on the water."

"The increased security does not surprise me, but I am not yet strong enough to make another attempt, even with your help. My throat was also damaged during the fight. But I have a question."

"I will answer if I can," the High Priest responded, not anticipating what would be asked.

"My nephew does not usually carry a weapon, but he was armed with the stick when I confronted him on the island. Did he have some warning that he was about to be attacked? Had you left any clues for him?"

Nebemakhet hesitated before replying. Was his loyalty now being doubted from both sides? "I can assure you that I did not let him have even the smallest hint of what you and I had discussed. He said that he needed the stick to help him walk over the rough ground, so one of the soldiers cut a branch for him. They even asked him if he wanted to be armed with a sword, but he declined the offer."

"Well, it is just out of character for him to have even a humble walking stick, although it did inflict significant damage on me." He then added, "I also want to be sure of your commitment in helping me achieve my goal. Are you still willing to assist me?"

Nebemakhet's ambition to become one of the gods was still burning within him. "Of course I am. What you have promised me if we succeed is all I need in return."

"Very well then," concluded Set. "We shall leave any further action until you have all returned to Memphis. Be alert for the next time I might wish to make contact with you."

Chapter 12. The homecoming

Imhotep had not been idle during the nearly eight weeks the Pharaoh had been away. He had been charged with investigating the feasibility of improving the Step Pyramid so that it would become a more powerful transmitter, or designing a bigger and better one. The existing structure had already been enhanced with a cladding of white limestone to create a smooth, gleaming surface, but it had only just succeeded in transporting the God of the Universe and his unwelcome companion. Neb-er-tcher had said that if he used it to return to his home world, or other deities tried to do so to visit Egypt, there was a risk of being mentally or physically damaged.

After taking careful measurements, the Vizier concluded that little more could be done with the present edifice. It had taken thousands of labourers nearly twenty years to build, and had used a third of a million stone blocks, but it was not the perfect. The base should have been exactly square, but he was now surprised to find that one side was longer than the other by a dozen paces. Some of the limestone was already coming loose and sliding away. If he tried to build the pyramid higher, the sides would be steeper and the cladding even more unstable. The best solution would be to build a bigger and better transmitter, but this would be expensive. What would the Pharaoh say?

It was late in the afternoon when the news came through that the barges carrying the royal party were nearing Memphis. Queen Hetephernebti was taken out to the landing stage to welcome her husband home. She was accompanied by General Intef and a contingent of soldiers for protection, along with transportation for the other members of the expedition. Djoser was the first to step on to the bank. "It is good to see you again," he said, embracing his wife.

"You have been away for a long time, and I have been looking forward to your safe return," the Queen replied.

"I have much to say to you," he said, as they walked toward their chariot. "But first, tell me, have there been any difficulties here in Memphis whilst we have been away?"

"The have been no serious incidences, but the people are very nervous about the presence of the Evil One. They think that Neb-er-tcher is to blame – and there is also some resentment against you for bringing him here."

The Pharaoh felt weary, and this showed in his face and bearing. He was now seventy-five years old, and had been reigning for twenty-seven of these. What he had hoped would be recorded as his finest achievement was now turning against him. "I have some good news to share," he said as cheerfully as he could. "Our mission to find out why the Nile does not flood has been successful, and we now know what we must do about it. Our citizens should have a better opinion of our guest when they hear this."

"I am sure they will," the Queen replied, as the chariot set off for their residence. "But do tell me everything about your trip. Did you encounter any difficulties?"

Djoser told her about the two attacks on Neb-er-tcher, and the loss of one of the soldiers. Hetephernebti was horrified to hear that Set had followed them along the river to pursue his murderous plan. Anyone could have been killed, including her husband.

"Is the God of Darkness still alive? If he is, do you know where he is now?" she asked.

"We have had no sight of him since the attack on the island. He may have perished, but the alien species appears to be superior to us in its ability to recover from serious injury. Until we know for certain, we must assume that he is still with us, and will again try to destroy his nephew."

They reached the palace with little more being said, each of them deep in thought about what needed to be done whilst the two aliens were here. There was much the Pharaoh knew he must address, now that he was back as Head of State, but that would have to wait until morning. To avoid unnecessary stops to replenish the provisions, the food on the barges had been meagre, even for the royal party. What he most needed now was an evening meal and some rest.

The next morning he sent for his key officials so he could be briefed on anything that needed his attention. He firstly summarised what had occurred during the expedition to Elephantine Island before stating: "The Queen has told me that there is anger among our people about the presence of the Evil One. How serious is this – do I have a rebellion on my hands?"

It was General Intef who responded first, diplomatically leading with a positive comment. "Your Majesty, the visible presence of soldiers on the streets has provided assurance to the citizens that they are being protected."

"I am pleased to hear this," Djoser replied. "Does this mean that everything is peaceful?"

"Unfortunately not, Sir. The people of Memphis have not forgotten the death of Guardsman Theshen, and they are unhappy that his killer is still roaming free. When they learn that one the soldiers on the barge has also been murdered, their hostility toward you may rise to a serious level."

"Would the knowledge that the God of the Universe was seriously injured by the Evil One reassure them that he is on our side?" the Pharaoh asked?

This time it was Abraxas the Chief Magistrate who responded. "Your Majesty, I doubt this will be sufficient. You appointed me as Executive Officer in your absence. In this capacity I have received several deputations from the people of Memphis and even beyond."

"This is unfortunate," Djoser interjected. "Do continue."

"There is a growing resentment about the time and money spent on building the Step Pyramid, and a fear that we have a monster loose in our land. Because Neb-er-tcher is of the same species as Set, he is starting to be regarded just as undesirable as is his evil uncle."

The Pharaoh realised that he would need to take action as quickly as possible, if he were to avoid an outright rebellion. He had hoped he would be remembered as the ruler who, with the help of the God of the Universe, had raised Egypt to a new level of power and prosperity. Instead, the possibility of him being deposed was looming, and his reputation could be destroyed for ever.

"Before this day is over, I shall address the people of Memphis and tell them how Neb-er-tcher discovered the cause of our periodic droughts, and what must be done when they occur. Surely this news will be received with rejoicing."

"Sir, I hope it will," Abraxas said. "If you were also able to tell them about other benefits that our alien guest will bestow on this land, that would strengthen your position even further."

"Very well, I shall discuss this with him before I speak to our citizens."

As he was also one of the Pharaoh's key officials, the High Priest was present at the meeting but had deliberately remained silent. His intention to aid Set and reap the promised reward remained strong. Hearing again the credit being given to Neb-er-tcher for discovering the reason for the Nile failing to flood only served to strengthen his resolve to help bring about the god's downfall. His thoughts were then rudely interrupted.

"Nebemakhet, you have spent much time with our guest, and you know him well," Djoser said. "What good news can I convey to the people concerning things he can do to help us?"

The High Priest had been placed in a difficult position, and needed to be careful with his response. "Sir, the two of us did talk many times during the voyage. Most of the conversation during the outward journey concerned the Nile flooding. I was pleased that he was able to use his powers to discover the cause of the droughts, and then suggest what actions could be taken. Because he was unfortunately injured whilst on the island, we spoke very little during the voyage home."

Had he sounded convincing? It took some effort to say anything complimentary about the being he was hoping would eventually be defeated.

The Pharaoh had expected more than this, and wondered if his official might not be revealing everything he knew. He would have to personally speak with Neb-er-tcher and try to obtain more examples of what he could do for them. Djoser then turned to the final member of the group, Chancellor Metjen. "What is the state of the treasury? Is our financial situation healthy?"

"Your Majesty, the cost of maintaining security has increased since the Evil One came here. You asked the General to ensure there was a visible presence of troops on the streets, and he had to call more men into service. We are still recovering from the cost of building the pyramid, as well as the effects of the drought that took place during that time."

"Are you saying we are running out of money?" the Pharaoh asked, with concern in his voice.

"No Sir, it is not as serious as that, at least not yet, but it would help if we can generate more revenue, or reduce our expenditure."

"Very well, I shall give this matter consideration. We can discuss this at a later time once more pressing matters have been dealt with. When we next meet, you must bring some suggestions of your own to help improve our finances."

Djoser brought the meeting to an end. He had much to do before he met the local citizens to try and calm the situation. It could escalate into a full-scale revolution if suitable action were not quickly taken. He now needed to speak with Imhotep, and asked one of his servants to go and find him.

"Sir, it is good to see you safely back home," the Vizier said. "I have not been idle whilst you have been away."

"Before I hear what you have done, I must tell you what we discovered about the Nile flood," the Pharaoh responded. "It is not under the control of Khumn on Elephantine Island, as we once thought."

"So what the High Priest did when he first visited was not responsible for the end of the drought?"

"Neb-er-tcher says it was just a coincidence, although it was good to renovate the temple there. The truth is that we have no control over the flooding, because it depends on the amount of snow and rainfall that falls far to the south."

Imhotep looked perplexed. "Does this mean we have to suffer, and risk starvation every time the falls there are light?"

"Certainly not," Djoser said. "The answer is to collect water when it is plentiful, and draw on this when it is scarce, just as we do with our grain."

"Of course, I can see now that this is the obvious thing to do. What do you wish of me so that it can be accomplished?"

"The ideal solution would be to build a giant dam at Aswan to hold the water back during the annual flood. It could then be released at the rate we need it without any wastage, and there will always be enough left when the deluge is low."

Imhotep thought carefully about the feasibility of such a project before answering. "Sir, it would be excellent if we could construct such a barrier, but I fear there would be difficulties we could not overcome, even if we had unlimited money and resources. Perhaps, many years hence, our descendents will have the knowledge and ability to succeed with such an undertaking, but it is not possible at this present time."

"Do not feel inadequate," the Pharaoh said sympathetically. "I had anticipated this would be the case, so instead I want you to design dams and reservoirs that can be constructed at all places along the Nile where the farmers grow their crops. These must fill up when the river is in flood, so that their contents can be stored, and used for irrigation during the droughts."

"I shall do as you ask," the Vizier replied. "Once the basic designs have been created, the farmers will be able to use them to build their own water storage facilities."

"Very well, I shall make sure copies of your plans are sent to all the farmers. There is another important matter I want to discuss with you. Before I embarked on my visit to Aswan, I asked you to consider ways of making the Step Pyramid more powerful. What can you tell me?"

"Sir, I have carefully reviewed the design, but it does not appear feasible to increase the power of the transmitter. If we build it higher, the sides will be steeper and the limestone cladding will not remain in place. Also, I have discovered that the base is not a perfect square. In order to make the pyramid bigger, and with equal sides, it would have to be demolished and re-built."

Djoser sighed; the bad news was continuing. "If we do not have a safe transmitter, both our alien visitors will be marooned here, and none of the other gods will be able to visit us. Are you intimating that we abandon our first pyramid and build a new one that is larger and more powerful?"

"That would be my recommendation," Imhotep replied. "We have learned much from our first attempt to construct such an edifice, and I am sure we would succeed with our second."

"I will have to find out if we can afford another major expenditure of this kind. In the meantime, go now and draw up your plans for a new transmitter. Even if we do have the money and manpower to build it, it will be many years before our guests from another universe will be able to return to their home."

Tiredness was again starting to envelop Djoser. The expedition to Aswan had been stressful and, now that they had all returned to Memphis, he was faced with opposition and possible rebellion. But he could not neglect his duties as both Head of State and spiritual leader. Before he addressed the citizens later in the day, he needed to meet with the God of the Universe and hear what additional benefits he could bring to the nation.

"Neb-er-tcher, it is good to see that you are now almost fully recovered from your unfortunate ordeal on the island."

"I must thank you for all the care and attention I have received from you and your people. Without this, I would surely have perished," the God replied.

With the pleasantries over, it was time for the Pharaoh to ask some serious questions. "You will have heard that the people are most unhappy about the deaths that have occurred at the hand of Set. Unfortunately, this is also reflecting badly on you, because you are of the same species as the Evil One."

"Yes, I heard these rumours as soon as we arrived back."

"I have promised to address the citizens later today," Djoser continued. "But I need some good news to tell them, otherwise we shall have a rebellion on our hands. You have already solved the mystery of why the Nile does not flood. What else can I tell them about the help you can give this nation to achieve greatness?"

Neb-er-tcher used his bony fingers to smooth the soft feathers on the back of his head, before responding with his musical chirping. "My species are more advanced than yours in many ways, including science, medicine, and building methods. We are the home of the gods, and the others could also help you if they were able to transport here safely."

"Yes, I do remember you telling me all this, but what can I say today that might convince the people that you are welcome to stay here?"

"You can tell them that I will immediately give instructions on how your body can be preserved when you die, so that you will be ready to enter the afterworld and enjoy the life that follows this one."

The Pharaoh looked pleased for the first time in many days. "Indeed, I am sure the citizens will welcome this news, and I hope it will dispel their desire to rise up against both you and me. But we still have the evil Set at large, and we do not yet have a reliable transmitter to transport either of you back to your home universe."

Djoser left Neb-er-tcher to continue his convalescence, and returned to his private chambers for some refreshment with Hetephernebti before addressing the crowd. "You are trying to do too much on your first full day back in Memphis," the Queen said, beckoning him to the chair next to her. "Come and enjoy your food, and tell me what you have learned."

Whilst they ate, the Pharaoh brought his wife up to date with what the others had said. When they had finished, he decided to rest for a short while after sending out the word that he would meet the crowds later that afternoon. Whether it was fatigue, or the goblet of wine, he soon fell asleep. Hetephernebti thought this was unusual for such a normally energetic man, but she let him slumber for an hour before waking him up.

"My husband, the people are waiting to hear what you have to say. Are you ready to meet them?

Djoser wearily roused himself. "Thank you for prompting me; I am ready to go now."

Judging from the numbers present, there could have been few inhabitants of Memphis who had avoided the opportunity to hear what their leader had to say.

"It is good to see so many of you here," the Pharaoh began, trying to maintain a strong and authoritative voice. "I have heard that you are concerned about the tragic deaths that have occurred recently. Well, so am I. In addition to these, when we were on Elephantine Island the God of the Universe was severely injured by the evil Set. He would have died had we not found him in time."

There were murmurings from the crowd, but it was difficult to know if they indicated sympathy for Neb-er-tcher, or regret that he survived.

"I am pleased to tell you that, thanks to our guest, the mystery of why the Nile sometimes fails to flood has been solved. We can

120

now take action to minimise the hardship that it causes during times of drought."

This news appeared to have been welcome, as no noises of dissent were forthcoming. "He also has many things to teach us," the Pharaoh continued, warming to his task. "His first action will be to show us how to preserve the body after death, so as to prepare it for a new life in the afterworld."

The people were clearly pleased to hear this, and exchanged approving comments. But then one man from the crowd shouted out: "Where is the evil Set now? Is he ready to kill again?" The mood suddenly changed to one of hostility.

"I do not know if he is alive or dead. Neb-er-tcher injured him during the fight on the island, and we have not heard or seen him since. But I can promise you that our troops will continue to patrol the streets to keep you all safe, and will make every effort to catch him if he is still at large."

Djoser hoped that this would be sufficient to avoid a rebellion. After a few more exchanges, the people dispersed. He had to keep his promises if he wanted to avoid another flare-up of anger, but further action would have to wait for another day. Exhaustion was now taking over his body. "I must retire to my bed to rest, even though it is not yet night," he told Hetephernebti when he reached palace. "There will be much to do tomorrow."

The Queen was surprised, but also concerned; her husband usually had more stamina than this. But these were difficult times, especially for an elderly ruler. "I understand," she said, resolving to keep checking on him to make sure all was well.

Hetephernebti slept fitfully, and awoke whilst it was still dark. She went over to where Djoser was lying on his bed. His body had grown cold; she listened for his breathing, but there was none; she tried to rouse him, but did not succeed.

Opening the door of their chambers she shouted out, "Come quickly, anyone who can hear me. The Pharaoh is dead!"

Chapter 13. The successor

Some of the servants heard the Queen's frantic cry, and came as quickly as they could. However, it was the God of the Universe who was the first to arrive. His mind had remained closely attuned to Djoser's, and he had sensed the life flow out of him.

"My dear husband is dead," Hetephernebti kept repeating, in between sobs. "He has only just returned from his trip, and we were looking forward to many more years together. Now he has gone."

Neb-er-tcher did not want to breach royal protocol, but he gently put his bony arm across the Queen's shoulders. "I share your grief," he said. "Your husband had become my friend. He had devoted twenty years of his reign to building the transmitter to bring me here. We had planned to do much to help your nation grow and prosper, but the work must still continue. It is what he would have wanted."

Hetephernebti became a little calmer. "What did he die of? Did the evil Set enter the palace during the night, and kill him?"

Neb-er-tcher examined the body for any sign of injury. "No, I do not believe he was murdered. He was seventy-five years old, and had just completed a stressful expedition to Aswan. As soon as he returned, he was faced with the threat of rebellion. My

123

judgement is that his body could not cope with all this at his age, and it just gave up."

By this time the servants had arrived, and were shocked to find their master dead. "Your Majesty, what do you wish us to do?" one of them asked.

The Queen was too distraught to issue a detailed list of instructions, but managed to say: "We shall just cover the body for now and leave it here until dawn. Then you must go to the houses of the senior officials and ask them to come to the palace urgently. But do not give them the reason, nor tell any of the citizens yet because we do not want to generate panic after yet another death."

The servants departed, and Hetephernebti sat down next to the lifeless body of her husband; unable to retain the composure she managed to muster whilst they were present, her sobbing now resumed even more intensely. "Would you like me to sit here with you?" Neb-er-tcher asked. The Queen just nodded, and there they remained, deep in their own thoughts, until daybreak.

Before the officials arrived, the Queen wrote three short notes, one to her daughter Inetkaes, and the others to Djoser's two brothers, Sekhemkhet and Sanakht, informing them of the Pharaoh's death. She asked them to come to the palace as soon as they could. Then, sending for her most trusted servant, she instructed him to saddle up one of the fastest horses and deliver these as quickly as possible.

The senior officials assembled in the throne room, and there was much speculation about why they had been suddenly sent for. The servants had obeyed the instruction not to reveal the reason for the meeting. When the Queen made her entrance, unaccompanied by her husband, some did start to wonder if the Pharaoh had been taken ill.

Drawing on all of her inner resources to try and remain composed at such a difficult time, Hetephernebti made her announcement. The initial reaction was one of stunned silence, but then everybody wanted to speak at once. Abraxas, the Chief Magistrate, who had been responsible for managing day-to-day affairs whilst the Pharaoh was away, was the first to make himself heard. "Your Majesty, this is indeed terrible news. Is there any evidence that he was murdered by the God of Darkness?"

"No, we do not believe this was the case," she replied. "Your leader had dedicated his life to doing what he believed was best for Egypt. But he was now elderly, and recent events had affected him deeply. He was worn out, and died peacefully in his sleep."

Again there was quiet, whilst those present absorbed the full impact of what had happened. General Intef then spoke. "This is sad news, both for the nation but also for you personally and your family. We have lost our Pharaoh, but you have lost your husband. May I offer you my deepest condolences. I know that the people will share the sadness of all of us when they hear the news. But the security patrols will continue to ensure that nobody can take advantage of the current situation."

One person who was not unhappy with what he had just heard was the High Priest. He had remained unsure about how much the Pharaoh had fully believed his version of events during the expedition to Aswan. Now that Djoser had departed this life, he felt free to continue with his traitorous plan to help the evil Set and reap the promised rewards. But he must be careful not to show this now.

"Your Majesty," he began, trying to sound sincere. "I am most saddened to hear of the passing of our wise and respected Pharaoh. As you know, I spent much time with him on the recent voyage, and I feel to have lost a friend as well as a leader. Please let me know how I can help you during this difficult time."

"I am most grateful for the kind words you have each expressed," the Queen said. "It is a comfort to me knowing that I have your loyalty and support. Members of my husband's family are expected to arrive here later today, and we shall discuss the funeral arrangements. There is also the urgent need to decide who shall succeed him."

Addressing General Intef, she continued: "I shall go now and compose a message to the people, informing them of what has happened, and assuring them that everything is under control. I would like your troops to distribute this throughout the land as quickly as they can."

With the meeting over, each person had duties to perform. The High Priest knew that he would be involved in the installation of a new Pharaoh, but hoped he would still be able to manipulate the situation to his own advantage. After all, no one would suspect he was working with the enemy, would they! He thought this would be an opportune time to try and make contact with Set again.

"God of Darkness, this is Nebemakhet," he said softly, once he was back in his own residence. Although he tried to project his words using only his mind, he still found it difficult to do so without speaking them. Would Set hear him? He had not had any contact with him since half way through the return voyage. Was he now back in Memphis, or had the injury he sustained from Neb-er-tcher's stick meant that he was still struggling to complete his journey?

He repeated his message throughout the day, without receiving a response. Deciding that he would try again the next day, he retired to bed. In the middle of the night he was woken up by what he thought was someone in the room talking to him, but once again the voice came from within his head. "This is Set. I have only just arrived in Memphis and found a safe place to hide. What do you wish to tell me?"

"I am glad you are back, and that your injury did not detain you for long. The important news is that Pharaoh Djoser has died. Some thought at first that it must have been your doing, but your nephew convinced the people that he had died of natural causes."

"I suppose I must be grateful to Neb-er-tcher for not taking the opportunity to put the blame me," Set said with a hint of sarcasm. "Do you know who will take his place?"

"No, not yet. But the Queen will meet with her family tomorrow to make a decision on his successor. It is customary that this role stays within the same blood-line, because the pharaohs are traditionally believed to be descendents of the gods."

Set's response again exhibited sarcasm. "You people of earth know nothing about the real gods. They all originate from my own universe, and none of them have become pharaohs! But we must talk about how I can defeat my nephew and take over his role as God of the Universe. That is, if you are still willing to help me."

"Of course I am," Nebemakhet said with some irritation. "But security is very high at this time. I suggest that we wait until after a new pharaoh has been appointed, and the situation has returned to normal. Then, I promise to try and arrange for you to confront Neb-er-tcher."

"Very well, I must take your word for this," Set replied. "But I shall grow impatient if kept waiting for too long. I came to your land on a mission, but have not yet succeeded in carrying it out. Do not contact me again until you have some useful news."

The transmission came to an abrupt end, just as the High Priest was about to seek reassurances about the reward promised to him for his help. He would have to be patient and wait for an opportunity to present itself to help the Evil One achieve his nefarious aim. Now that Djoser was dead, at least he was free of the worry that his conduct during the Aswan trip may have aroused some suspicion. His secret liaison with Set was now safe.

But he was wrong. Someone else had a very clear notion of what was going on. It was only when Set contacted Nebemakhet that the God of the Universe detected the transmissions. His species had evolved the ability to monitor communications going on around them, just as humans can hear the background hubbub of conversations. Mostly these are ignored but, when we hear our name, or perhaps a cry for help, we immediately pay attention.

So his uncle was still alive, as he had suspected, and remained intent on defeating him. And Nebemakhet was still willing to help. It was useful to know this, but he decided to continue to keep this knowledge to himself, at least for the present. As had been the case on Elephantine Island, he would be alert to any attack that would be made on him.

It was Inetkaes, the Queen's daughter who was the first to arrive at the royal residence the next day, accompanied by her husband Itju. Putting her arms around her mother, and trying to hold back her sobbing, she said, "We came as quickly as we could. Poor father, I am so sorry. I hope he did not suffer."

There was only a little time for consolations before the other family members joined them. After some further tearful embraces, Sekhemkhet, the eldest of Djoser's siblings, said: "We came as quickly as we could. It is tragic that Sanakht and I have lost our beloved brother and Pharaoh. He was in good health the last time we saw him. Please tell us what happened. Was he attacked?"

"No," the Queen replied. "My husband died peacefully in his sleep. As you know, he was not a young man, and was very weary after he returned from Aswan. But he had no time to rest; the people of Memphis were threatening to rebel. They are unhappy about the recent deaths that have occurred, for which both of our alien visitors are held responsible."

"Did the crowd threaten my brother?" Sekhemkhet asked.

"No. He managed to placate the gathered throng for the time being, telling them about some of the helpful things that Neb-ertcher can do for this nation and all who live here."

Sanakht then spoke. "But do we still have the evil Set at large, ready to kill again?"

"Unfortunately yes, at least we think he is still alive," Hetephernebti said. "But your brother vowed that every effort would be made to capture him. In the meantime, the troops will continue to patrol the streets to keep the people safe. These promises must be fulfilled by whoever becomes the next pharaoh."

Inetkaes had been listening carefully to what the others had been saying. Although still trying to come to terms with the loss of her father, she felt it was important to raise a pertinent issue. "Mother, you just said what the next pharaoh must do, but who will this be?"

"As you know, it is customary for the role be retained within the royal family," the Queen began. "Only if there are no siblings or children do we look elsewhere. There are four of us here who would be eligible to succeed my husband, but my belief is that the next pharaoh should be his eldest brother, Sekhemkhet. Does anyone disagree?"

"Indeed, he is the obvious choice, and I support his nomination," said the younger Sanakht.

Inetkaes was also in agreement, so Hetephernebti now directed a question directly at Sekhemkhet. "Are you willing to be the next leader of this land?" she asked.

"This will be an awesome responsibility, especially during these troubled times," he replied. "But I accept that it is my destiny, and agree to take on this appointment."

"Very well," the Queen continued. "I shall ask the High Priest to arrange the inauguration as soon as possible. The people need to see that we have a strong leader in place who can guide the nation through its current difficulties."

"Mother, when my cousin and his family take up residence in this palace, I would like you to come and live with my husband Itju and me," Inetkaes said. "It will be good for you to be away from the situation here in Memphis, and have time to enjoy your retirement."

"Thank you, that is very kind of you my daughter; I will be happy to leave this place and come to stay with you. But now you must all go and rest after your journey, and take some refreshment. I need to make arrangements for the funeral, and shall join you later."

Neb-er-tcher was waiting outside the door, and asked to see the Queen as soon as the others had left. "Your Majesty," he began, "may I speak with you?"

"Of course, you are always welcome," Hetephernebti replied, beckoning him toward the chair next to her. "What do you wish to discuss with me?"

"Your late husband will have told you that I am willing to reveal how to preserve the body, in order to prepare it for the afterlife." The Queen nodded. "Well," he continued, "I think it would be good to start with Pharaoh Djoser himself. Not only will his accomplishments be remembered until eternity, but the earthly body that he has left behind will be there for all to see."

"That is a wonderful suggestion, and I am sure the family will agree with me in giving their approval," she responded.

"If we do this, we shall have to start the process tomorrow whilst the body is still fresh. But I have yet a further proposal," Neb-er-tcher continued. "The Step Pyramid, for which he dedicated many years of his reign in building in order to bring me here, is a magnificent structure. It is just unfortunate that it has proved to be unreliable as a transmitter."

"Yes, I am aware of its limitations," Hetephernebti commented. "Are you going to suggest making some changes to it?"

"No, not in the way you may be thinking, but I would like to propose that the underground chamber becomes the burial place of your late husband. From that time onwards, it will be known as Pharaoh Djoser's tomb."

The Queen felt tears start to form in her eyes again, not just of sorrow but mingled with joy at the thought that the memory of her beloved husband would be preserved in this way. "Thank you so much for your inspiring ideas," she managed to reply. "I shall discuss these with the other members of the family when I meet with them for refreshments in a little while. But firstly I must see the High Priest to arrange the inauguration of Sekhemkhet as the new Pharaoh."

With the ceremony now scheduled for three days hence, Hetephernebti joined the other family members and gave them the latest news. There were no objections to what the God of the Universe had suggested. Like Hetephernebti, they were both pleased and comforted to know that Djoser would be remembered in such a fitting manner.

The next morning, they all met with Neb-er-tcher at the mortuary to hear how he was going to preserve the late leader's body. He had also requested that Nebemakhet and two of the assistant priests be present. "I shall teach you what must be done," he began. "But it is not for the faint-hearted. The work is usually carried out by the clergy, and the relatives may decide not to witness it until it has been completed."

The family members found this strange. Sekhemkhet, who was already adopting the senior role, asked on behalf of them all: "What is going to happen that we might not want to watch?"

"Firstly, most of his internal organs will be removed, and placed in a jar. If left where they are, they will cause his body to putrefy. Only his heart will remain in place. Then he will be covered in natron salt and left for several weeks until the flesh has completely dried. After that, his body will be washed and then carefully wrapped with layers of cloth. Some warm resin will be added before the final shroud is tied in place."

"I can understand why you warned us that we might not want to witness this," Hetephernebti said. "I think I would like to remember my husband as he was, rather than watch him be butchered as you have described." Out of respect for the Queen, the others also agreed to leave the embalming process to the priestly cast, and quietly withdrew from the mortuary.

The family's energies were now directed toward the inauguration of Sekhemkhet. Hetephernebti did not want to leave the nation without a strong leader during these troubled times. She had already decided not to wait until dignitaries from neighbouring countries could arrive, or even those from the more remote parts of Egypt. A simple ceremony would have to suffice, held outside so as many of the local populous as possible could witness the event.

A small platform was erected in the palace courtyard and, two days later, the formalities took place. The Queen opened the proceeding: "Citizens of Memphis, we are still in mourning for the death of your king, Pharaoh Djoser, but today we celebrate the investiture of a new head of State, his brother Sekhemkhet. I ask you to be as loyal and faithful to him as you were to my late husband."

Nebemakhet the High Priest then put the royal robe around Sekhemkhet's shoulders and the crown upon his head. An anointing of oil on the forehead, and some incantations, completed the procedure.

The new Pharaoh then faced the crowd. "I am honoured to be your new leader. My brother worked hard all of his life to make this country great, and I shall do the same. There are many things awaiting my attention, so I ask you to be patient. We are all concerned that there is an evil being at large in our land, but we shall hunt him down without mercy. I ask you to continue your normal activities, but remain alert. Our soldiers will maintain their presence on the streets."

With that, the inauguration was over, and the crowd started to disperse. Out of sight in his hiding place nearby, Set was amused to hear that he would be hunted down without mercy, but his avian face was incapable of forming a smile. Who would triumph in the end remained to be seen.

Chapter 14. The plan

Sekhemkhet knew the situation in Memphis required his immediate attention, and he had little time to spend on the domestic chores of moving into the royal residence. He therefore asked his wife, Djeseretnebti, and their son Khaba to organise the transfer of their personal belongings into the palace, whilst he took up temporary residence in one of the guest rooms.

The new Pharaoh was only three years younger than Djoser. His facial features were less prominent than those of his predecessor, and he welcomed the opportunities to hide his receding chin with the strip of false beard that it was customary to wear on formal occasions.

After assuring himself that the security patrols were maintaining a visible presence on the streets, both day and night, to give reassurance to the citizens, one of the first people he wished to speak with was Imhotep.

"Your Majesty," the Vizier said, as soon as he had been admitted to the chambers, "it will be an honour to serve you as Pharaoh, just as I did your late brother. Tell me what you wish of me."

"Thank you, Imhotep. My brother often told me how skilled you are in many things. You are a most valuable member of this nation, and I know you will be of great help to me."

The Vizier was a modest man, and compliments always caused him some embarrassment. Nevertheless, he was pleased that his relationship with the new Head of State appeared to be making such a good start. But, with the introductory pleasantries now over, Sekhemkhet turned to more serious matters.

"Imhotep, I know something of the pyramid you built to transport the God of the Universe to this land, but tell me what the current situation is."

"Sir, the Step Pyramid at Saqqara is not reliable enough to use again without risk of injury, so both our alien visitors will be marooned here until we can construct something more powerful."

"Is it not possible to improve the structure we already have?"

"I have considered this very carefully but, unfortunately, it will become unstable if we try to build it higher. However, we could demolish the whole edifice and use the stone blocks to build a new one."

Although Sekhemkhet saw this as the most obvious solution, he knew that it could not be done. "I agree that this would be a possibility, but it has been decided that the pyramid will become the final resting place of our late Pharaoh. It will be known for ever as Djoser's Tomb."

Imhotep nodded in approval. "It is appropriate that the construction he did so much to bring to fruition will become a permanent monument to his greatness. Your brother did ask me to consider all possibilities, and I have drawn up plans for a new transmitter that should overcome the shortcomings of the first one."

"Excellent. Tell me more about this. Will it also be a pyramid?"

"Yes Sir; it is the shape that Neb-er-tcher requires. This time the base will be perfectly square, and it will be over ten metres higher and thus steeper. The sides will be constructed so that the limestone cladding will fit into recesses and not fall off."

Sekhemkhet considered this information for a few moments before commenting: "The Step Pyramid took twenty years to complete. It seems to me that the second one will take at least as long."

"There are several reasons why I am sure it will be done much quicker this time," Imhotep responded. "We now have much more knowledge about how to build these large structures, and will not make the same mistakes as we did last time."

"I am also aware that, if we do embark on a new transmitter, we now have the God of the Universe to advise us," the Pharaoh added.

"That will certainly be a great help. Also, I know that many more stone blocks were cut from the Great Trench than we used last time, so we would be able to make a start almost immediately. I have located a suitable site at Saqqara a few hundred metres southwest of the Step Pyramid, so the labourers could use the same accommodation we originally provided for them."

"Very well, I will now consult with Chancellor Metjen to see if we have sufficient funds to undertake another major building project. I shall also arrange for you to meet with Neb-er-tcher so you can show him your plans."

Imhotep then departed, and Sekhemkhet firstly went to see how the mummification of Djoser was progressing, so he would know when to schedule the interment. He then sent for the Chancellor to question him on the state of the treasury.

"Sir," Metjen began, "our finances are similar to what they were when the first pyramid was constructed. We can afford to make a start on the new building, but we need to ensure that our coffers are being continuously replenished through taxes, exports, and the spoils of war. If our revenue falls, then we shall have to cease working on this expensive project."

"I understand," the Pharaoh said. "The God of the Universe came to help us in many ways, so he must now honour his promise and tell us how this land of Egypt can become more powerful and prosperous."

"Indeed, if we can generate even more money, then we shall have no difficulty in underwriting prestigious ventures such as the pyramid."

"Very well, I shall ask the Vizier to make a start on the new transmitter, and continue with it unless you advise me that our finances are running low."

Sekhemkhet's final activity of this busy day – his first after taking on the full responsibilities of office – was to send for the High Priest to make arrangements for the funeral of his late brother.

"Nebemakhet, you will be aware that my brother's body will be entombed in the pyramid to which he had dedicated twenty years of his reign."

"Your Majesty, it is an excellent idea, and a fitting memorial to our dearly beloved leader," he replied, trying to sound sincere.

"Good. But I want the ceremony to be equally fitting. It will be your responsibility to compile a suitable order of service and then bring it to me for approval. As High Priest, you will then officiate at the internment."

"It will be an honour to do this," Nebemakhet responded, confident that the one person who might have suspected his secret liaison with the Evil One was no longer able to betray him. "Do you have a date when this will take place?"

"Yes, the preparation of the body for the afterlife will have been completed exactly four weeks from now. The ceremony must be held on that day."

The High Priest left to start work on the burial service. As he had received word of what had been planned and, as officiant, that he would be in a position to influence the proceedings, it was a suitable time to contact Set again. He had been told not to do so unless he had news that could be used to help defeat his adversary, but his alien partner would surely be interested in what he could now tell him.

When evening came he retired to his bed chamber and spoke softly, trying to project his thoughts as he did so. "God of Darkness, this is Nebemakhet. Can you hear me?" As was usually the case, he had to repeat his message several times, and then wait for a response. Eventually it came, but he was not the only one who heard it.

"Nebemakhet, this is Set. I can hear you. Do you have something useful to tell me; something that will help me in my mission?"

"Yes, I have some important information. Twenty-eight days from now the Step Pyramid will be unsealed, and the mummified body of Pharaoh Djoser will be interred in the underground chamber. It will then be permanently resealed to deter grave robbers."

"Does this mean that no attempt will be made to make it into a more reliable transmitter?"

"That is correct. It seems that it will become unstable if it is enlarged. Plans have been drawn up for a new building, which will be built in the desert a short distance away from what will become the late Pharaoh's tomb."

Set made noises that, even in the alien tongue, sounded suspiciously like curses. "But a new transmitter will take many years to build. Am I to be marooned in this inhospitable land of yours for the next twenty years?"

Nebemakhet tried to placate his clearly angry associate. "I am told that the new structure will be completed much more quickly than was the Step Pyramid; some stone blocks are already available, and the infrastructure still remains."

"We shall have to see," Set responded. "But tell me how the burial of Djoser is going to help me to achieve my goal – and I should remind you that your own reward will depend on my success."

"I certainly have not forgotten the promise you made to me. There will only be room for a few people in the pyramid chamber – probably just the family members, Neb-er-tcher, and one or two servants to carry the body. I shall also be present, leading the service."

"Are you saying that, during this time, you will be able to create an opportunity for me to attack my nephew?"

"That is my plan. You should have the chance to enter the chamber when it has been unsealed, and find a hiding place down there. When the formalities have been completed, I shall try to divert Neb-er-tcher so that he will be last of the group to leave. That will be your chance to strike, just as you did when you came through the transmitter, and despatched Guardsman Theshen."

"Indeed, what you have described is a possibility," conceded Set. "There just remains the small matter of how I make my escape, once I have completed my task. Surely there will be many people waiting outside the pyramid on such an auspicious occasion."

"That would be to your advantage," Nebemakhet responded. "When it is noticed that Neb-er-tcher has not emerged from the chamber, several people will go back down to try and find him. Once they see him lying dead, there will be pandemonium. Guards and other officials will be rushing in and out, removing the body and trying ascertain what happened. This should be your chance to slip away, especially if you are able to disguise yourself."

"Very well, I shall consider what you have told me, and make my attempt if I am confident of succeeding. But you must play your part and not let me down, otherwise there will be no reward for you."

"You can be assured that I have as much desire as you have in ensuring that this plan will succeed," the High Priest replied, wondering if the God of Darkness still did not have complete confidence in him.

"I shall go now," Set replied. "Do not contact me again before the entombment, unless something happens to interfere with our plans. I do not want to risk our conversations being overheard."

He was right to consider this possibility, but too late to prevent an eavesdropper from hearing exactly what was being planned.

This latest discussion between the Evil One and Nebemakhet did not come as a surprise to the God of the Universe. He suspected there would be another attempt to attack him, and now he knew both when and where. There was still nearly a month before Djoser's internment, so he had plenty of time to decide what he would do about it.

Up to now he had kept his knowledge of the High Priest's complicity to himself but, if this latest attempt was to be thwarted, he must now confide in others. The new Pharaoh had been busy trying to cope with all the difficulties he had inherited, and Neb-er-tcher had had little contact with him. But he would be the appropriate person with whom to share what he had just overheard. If this led to the capture of the murderous Set, it would give a welcome boost to Sekhemkhet's reputation. He would seek an appointment with him.

"God of the Universe, I regret that our only meeting so far was in the mortuary, when you instructed the priests in the art of mummification," Sekhemkhet said as he directed his visitor toward a chair. "There has been much that has demanded my immediate attention, and I have had to put aside anything that is not urgent. But the situation now seems to be stable, at least for the moment, so I welcome this chance to discuss matters with you."

"Thank you, Pharaoh," Neb-er-tcher replied. "Have you been apprised of the status of the transmitter that enabled me to come to your kingdom?"

Sekhemkhet had not yet become proficient in the technique of ignoring the musical chirps that came from the alien's mouth, and concentrating on the voice that entered directly into his mind. "If I have correctly interpreted what you have asked, then yes, the Step Pyramid was unreliable and a new one will be built. This means that you will probably be with us for a few more years."

"Yes, that may be the case. But I came here to help this nation become more advanced and prosperous, and that is what I can do until a new transmitter is available."

"I welcome this, and look forward to hearing more about your proposals. Is there anything you immediately wish to share with me?"

"Sir, there is another matter of great importance that we need to discuss now," Neb-er-tcher replied.

"Please go on," Sekhemkhet urged.

"I have reason to believe that Set will make an attack on my life during the internment of your brother's body in the underground chamber."

It took a few moments for the full impact of this news to register with the Pharaoh. "How do you know this?" he asked.

"Just as my words are being projected into your mind as we face each other, my species has developed the ability to communicate over longer distances. It is possible for others to intercept these conversations, just as you humans can sometimes overhear what others are saying."

"So you have been eavesdropping on some traitorous individual? Tell me who this is, and I shall immediately have him captured."

"Sir, I have not been listening to one of your kind, but to my Uncle, Set. He followed me through the transmitter so that he could destroy me, and he will try to do so again when we are down in the chamber."

Sekhemkhet was still trying to assimilate the significance of what he had just been told. "Of course, we shall have many guards with us, and this will ensure your protection."

"When he sees the extra security, he will realise that his intentions have been overheard, and will likely abort his attempt to kill me. It is to our advantage that he does not suspect this, and I respectfully suggest that you tell no one about what I have learned. Let this be a secret between just the two of us."

"If that is what you wish, I will certainly honour your request. But how are you going to resist the attack?"

"I shall give some more thought to that," Neb-er-tcher replied. "But my aim will be to create an opportunity for your guardsmen to capture Set alive. Just think how the citizens will rejoice when you display him in chains for all to see. They will sing your praises as the one who has rid them of this evil monster."

Sekhemkhet was visibly pleased to hear how he could attain favour among his subjects so early in his reign. The thought of this banished any intention he might have had to ask with whom the Evil One had been speaking. Neb-er-tcher had already decided not to reveal the treacherous involvement of the High Priest just yet. He would eventually be exposed but, for now, it could prove an advantage to keep his name clear.

"Sir, may I again request that you tell nobody of this development. If Set is to be captured, we cannot risk even the slightest chance that he might suspect his plan is known."

The Pharaoh was still feeling happy at the prospect of such a boost to his reputation. "Of course; if that is your recommendation, then I agree. We still have plenty of time to make our arrangements, so I ask you to come and see me again when you have decided on your strategy."

Neb-er-tcher withdrew from the royal chambers, and returned to his own quarters to devote time to formulating a plan that had a good chance of succeeding. Key to the whole operation would be the surprise element. However, Sekhemkhet and he could not accomplish this by themselves; others would have to know at some time before the internment.

By the time dawn broke the next day, he was confident he knew what should be done. The Step Pyramid had been sealed immediately following the death of Guardsman Theshen, but it would have to be reopened to prepare it for the ceremony. Craftsmen had been busy carving a sarcophagus from a single stone block and this, with its lid, would have to be manoeuvred down into the burial chamber. Set would have plenty of opportunity to enter the building and find a hiding place.

Pallbearers would be needed to carry the mummified body as well as items of food, clothing, and furniture the late Pharaoh would need in the afterlife. When he reported back to Sekhemkhet, Neb-er-tcher would suggest that all these extra helpers be soldiers in disguise. They would be briefed just prior to entering the chamber, and told to be prepared for an attack that would be made when people were leaving at the close of the ceremony.

The preparation of the late Pharaoh's remains for burial was eventually completed. By the time the royal party arrived at the pyramid for the internment, many people had assembled outside to pay their last respects to the late Pharaoh. The High Priest led the group down into the already lighted chamber. He was followed by two assistants carrying the body on a bier, and four soldiers in disguise bearing the accoutrements for the next life. The family members came next, along with Neb-er-tcher. Last to enter were two more soldiers in servant clothes, holding torches.

When all had taken their places inside the chamber, Nebemakhet began with incantations for the departed one. Djoser's mummified body was reverently lifted into the sarcophagus, and personal items of clothing and jewellery were placed on top of it. Finally, the lid was slid into place. Hetephernebti had remained impassive up to this point, but tears now started to flow. Inetkaes put her arms around her mother, whilst trying to control her own emotion, and she and Itju gently guided her out of the chamber.

The remainder of the group started to follow at a respectful distance but, as Neb-er-tcher began to move away, the High Priest stopped him. Taking the torch from the last of the bearers and handing it to him, he said, "It would be appropriate for you to say a final prayer, calling on your gods to care for our beloved Pharaoh in the next life."

This did not come as a surprise, and it was also what Set had been waiting for as he watched the events from his hiding place in a side passage. As the God of the Universe stood alone in front of the tomb, the Evil One leapt out and launched himself at Neb-er-tcher. But his nephew was ready for this, and thrust the blazing torch into the face of his adversary.

There was no time for another attempt as four of the guards, who had been waiting in the dark just outside the chamber, rushed back inside and overpowered Set. They bound his arms to his sides and led him along the passage to the outside. The crowds were just starting to disperse when they heard gleeful shouts coming from the pyramid entrance: "We have him! The God of Darkness has been captured!"

Chapter 15. The Rods of Horus

What had started as a solemn occasion suddenly changed into one of rejoicing. Set stood at the entrance of the pyramid, his facial feathers singed by the flaming torch, forcibly constrained by the four smiling guardsmen who were now free of their servant disguises.

The first reaction of the people, who were now streaming back to see what the commotion was about, was one of shock. The image that most of them had formed in their minds of the evil monster that had killed two of their number was of a large and powerful beast. What they saw was a slender figure with a head like an ibis and its long, curved beak. Although Set's beady, black eyes defiantly returned their stares, it was difficult to believe that this creature was indeed responsible for the recent murders.

After gazing at the alien for some time, and passing comments among themselves, the mood of the crowd started to change. It began with a few individuals shouting insults, and it then escalated into anger. The people started to move forward, screaming for revenge and demanding that the Evil One be executed immediately. General Intef, who had so successfully prepared the guards for their role in Set's capture, had to muster all available soldiers in the area to help hold back the throng.

It needed somebody to bring calm to the situation. Pharaoh Sekhemkhet strode confidently to where the alien was being held, and turned to address the gathering. "Citizens of Egypt, it is fitting that the capture of this wicked creature has occurred whilst we were gathered to remember my late brother. His anxiety about the God of Darkness being still at large, ready to kill again, added to his exhaustion. I am sure this contributed to his untimely death, but he can now rest in peace."

Someone from the crowd shouted: "Let us kill the alien."

Others took up the chant and very quickly there was a chorus of, "Kill the alien! Kill the alien!" The people started to press forward again, and the soldiers had to use all their combined strength to prevent Set from being torn from their hands.

The Pharaoh raised his hands and called out as loudly as he could: "Calm down; calm down, my friends. Taking revenge on the prisoner in this way is not the answer."

Although it was impossible to read the expression on Set's avian face, his body language betrayed an obvious fear that he was about to meet a brutal end at the hands of a very angry mob. He tried to shrink away as the crowd advanced, and had to twist and turn to avoid being seized. What did the Pharaoh have in mind for him? he wondered.

Sekhemkhet continued. "The God of Darkness will be taken away and cast into our most secure dungeon. He will be guarded day and night by our soldiers, and will never escape. We shall then try him for his crimes. If he is found guilty, he may be sentenced to be executed, and you will have the pleasure of witnessing this."

These words had the desired effect of easing the tension among the onlookers, and they fell back. However, the mention of execution did little to please the Evil One. At least he now had some time in which to try and plan an escape, but he would make sure that the High Priest played his part in this if he expected to be rewarded.

After letting the crowd have its fill of hurling insults at Set, the prisoner was led away to be incarcerated, and the people started to disperse. Even though Sekhemkhet had been forewarned of the attack, he was nevertheless curious to know how events played out in the tomb after he had left it. He called the key players together for a briefing.

"Nebemakhet, you and Neb-er-tcher were the last to leave the chamber. Tell us what happened."

"Your Majesty, the God of the Universe took the torch from me and went up to the sarcophagus to offer a final prayer to his own gods. I was respectfully standing back in the shadows, and did not see Set until he made his attack. Fortunately, my companion was able to use the flaming lamp to defend himself. The guards then appeared surprisingly quickly."

"I see. It is fortunate that the soldiers were not far away, otherwise the Evil One might have had a second chance," the Pharaoh said, knowing full well that this is what had been secretly arranged. "Let us now hear what Neb-er-tcher has to say."

"The High Priest has described accurately what happened. I am glad I had the torch in my hand, and grateful to the guards for immediately coming to my aid." Although he could have cast some suspicion on Nebemakhet, he still maintained his resolve not to do so; being able to intercept the communications between him and Set had already proved its worth.

Sekhemkhet finally called the senior guardsman to hear his story. He had been party to the plan to thwart the attempt on Neb-er-tcher's life, but was playing his role well.

"Your Majesty, I was with my men who were leaving the chamber after helping to carry the burial artefacts and seal the sarcophagus. We knew that the God of the Universe and the High

Priest were still down there, so we waited in the passage ready to escort them out when they were ready to leave."

The Pharaoh encouraged the guard to continue. "What happened next?"

"Sir, we heard a noise, and turned to look. It was then that we saw the God of Darkness holding his face. We rushed back into the chamber and seized him."

"You and your men did well, and you shall be rewarded for capturing the Evil One," Sekhemkhet said. "You may go now, but do not let your prisoner escape."

The smiling guardsman departed, and the royal party returned to Memphis. It had been an eventful day, and they each had their own thoughts about the implications of Set being locked up and no longer a threat to the community – assuming he stayed that way.

Whilst the Pharaoh and Neb-er-tcher were delighted that their secret plan had been successful, the High Priest was not so pleased. Once again an attempt on the life of the God of the Universe had failed, and once again he had to be very careful not to allow himself to be implicated. He had managed to do this so far, or so he thought, but he would surely be exposed if there were another failure. Should he try to contact Set? Perhaps not straight away, he decided; best to let the situation settle down first.

The thought of what should be done with the God of Darkness was also on Neb-er-tcher's mind when he met Imhotep at the building site to discuss the design of the new pyramid. Sending his uncle back to his own world was not a viable option at this time.

"You have made some important improvements, and these should overcome the unreliability we experienced with the first transmitter," he said, after scrutinising the plans and pointing with a claw-like finger.

"I am pleased that you approve of my proposal," the Vizier replied. "I realised how important it was for the base to be perfectly square, and it is unfortunate that what has become the final resting place of our late Pharaoh had deviated from this by twelve paces."

"Yes, you are correct. The secret is for the building to be completely symmetrical in every direction. Transmitting people from one universe to another is no easy achievement, and the signal must not be corrupted by any irregularities in the structure."

"I do understand this now," Imhotep said, his frame clad, only in the wrap-around skirt, clearly showing him as a man of action. Always ready for new challenges and experiences, he added: "It is a wonderful thing that your species is able to do; how exciting it would be if we earthlings could also travel in this way."

Neb-er-tcher attempted a human smile, but his hawk-like beak only twisted into something that looked more grotesque than agreeable. "It has taken us thousands of years to perfect this procedure. Perhaps your species will succeed one day, but it carries a big responsibility. It is not a pathway to self-gain or domination, despite what you have experienced with Set. Our mission as gods is to help other civilisations to advance, and to bring peace and prosperity to all whom we visit. Would the people of earth follow these same goals if they could travel to other worlds?"

"I am no philosopher, but I am certain we are as yet too immature in our development to embrace your altruistic principles," the Vizier admitted. "In our society, the leaders devote most of their efforts to expanding their own empires so that they can become still more rich and powerful. The idea of helping weaker nations to overcome their difficulties, without seeking any reward, is not yet something that motivates many individuals here."

Neb-er-tcher brought the conversation back to the main reason for their discussion. "I see no reason to make any changes to your plans for the new pyramid. When will you be able to start, and how long will it take? Remember that I will not be able to return to my own world without a dependable transmitter."

"Sir, this project will be accomplished far more quickly than was the case with our first one. We still have some stone blocks remaining that we can put in place immediately. Captain Meru has already been despatched to the Great Trench at Aswan to mobilise the quarrymen. Also, our labourers now have experience in building such a structure. Perhaps, with your own knowledge, you can help us to complete the project more quickly and efficiently than before."

"Indeed I shall do that, and there is one suggestion I can make immediately. But first, tell me, how did you transport the heavy stones the fifteen kilometres from the landing stage on the Nile to the building site?"

"It was a slow process," Imhotep replied. "We dragged them across the desert on wooded sledges, one block at a time. Many labourers were involved. We tried using rollers but they did not help because they just sank into the soft sand."

"Then you might wish to consider digging a canal from the Nile to Saqqara. Just make it wide enough for one barge at a time, provided you include some passing places. The channel would not need to be built to last, and could be filled in again once the new pyramid had been completed."

"That is an excellent idea," the Vizier said enthusiastically. "It will save us much time and effort. I shall consult with the Pharaoh to obtain his approval. If he agrees, we can temporarily divert labour from the pyramid building and make an urgent start on the water channel."

"Good, I am pleased you think this will be a help to you. But I have just one more point to add for the moment. You will still have to drag the blocks short distances. Make sure that the sand in front of the sledges is first soaked with water, and you will find they pull along much more easily."

With that, Neb-er-tcher left Imhotep to continue his work at the building site, and returned to his quarters at the royal residence. The sooner the new transmitter was completed, the greater the number of options there would be both for his own future and that of his uncle.

After all the activity and excitement of the last few weeks, life in Memphis returned to what a visitor to the town may have regarded as a calm and orderly existence. People went about their business, feeling safe to be out on the streets now that the Evil One had been incarcerated. But, if the stranger paid a visit to the Vizier's house, he or she would see the frenetic activity of a man trying to cope with several major projects at once.

The Pharaoh had needed little convincing to appreciate the merits of building the canal, and had readily given his approval. In addition to supervising its construction, Imhotep made a start on the pyramid itself, using the materials remaining from the first structure. Then there was the water conservation programme to build dams and reservoirs along the Nile. Fortunately, once he had drawn up the plans, they could be taken to individual farms by assistants who would then provide whatever help was needed.

It had been an eventful start to Sekhemkhet's reign, but it was fortuitous that the capture of Set so early in his tenure had resulted in him being quickly accepted as leader by the citizens. Once he had become familiar with the duties that his role required, and presided over several briefings with his key advisers, it was time for him to try and advance his own reputation and that of the nation over which he ruled. He asked Neb-er-tcher to come and see him.

"What are we going to do about your uncle?" was the Pharaoh's opening question. "We can keep him locked up indefinitely, but this is not our usual practice. Prisoners either reach the end of their sentences and are released, or they are executed."

"I would not recommend execution," the god replied, settling his two-metre frame into the chair he had been offered. "He is ultimately my responsibility and, once again, I regret that he has been imposed upon you. When we have a reliable transmitter, I shall try to send him back to my universe where he can be dealt with by the Supreme God, Ra. Until then, he must continue to be kept out of harm's way."

"Very well, this will be done, and we shall devote all our efforts toward building the new pyramid. But there is something else I need to ask you."

"I will answer if I can," Neb-er-tcher responded. He had a suspicion that it might concern the name that so far he had failed to divulge.

Sure enough, the Pharaoh said: "You have been intercepting messages from your uncle, but with whom has he been communicating?"

"Indeed I have been secretive about this up to now, because it has been useful for me to eavesdrop on the conversations. It is Nebemakhet the High Priest."

"This does not surprise me," Sekhemkhet commented. "From what I have seen and heard, he has always been there during Set's attacks. Sometimes he has been the only witness. Should I have him immediately arrested? Whilst he remains free, he might try to help your uncle escape, with potentially disastrous consequences – especially for you."

"It is a difficult decision. But he still does not think anyone suspects his treachery. If he is taken prisoner it will deprive Set of his only ally, and then I would have no way of intercepting messages that inform us of what mischief is being planned."

"Very well," the Pharaoh replied, fingering his false beard. "If you think it will be useful to let him remain free for the time being, we shall do so. But now I want to ask you about what more you can do to help Egypt become more powerful and prosperous. You have told us that this was your purpose for coming to our land."

"That was indeed my reason for choosing your nation among all others on this earth. You will know that I have already discovered the reason why the Nile sometimes fails to flood, and what can be done to conserve the water. Then I have shown you how to preserve the body after death in order to prepare it for the afterlife. My latest advice was to Imhotep on the construction of the canal that will enable the stone blocks to be brought directly onto the building site."

"Yes, these are excellent things you have done for us," Sekhemkhet agreed. "But have you any other suggestions, especially ones that will impress the people and enhance my reputation?"

Neb-er-tcher was not impressed by the motivation for the Pharaoh's question, as the purpose for his assistance was to benefit everyone, and not just the current Head of State. The human race was clearly not as morally advanced as he had hoped it would be. Nevertheless, he did not want to upset his host. "I can tell you about a magical product that was created by the god Horus, and which can only be made inside the pyramid."

"Do please continue, I am eager to hear more about this," the Pharaoh said, clearly intrigued by the mention of 'magical'.

"Fine white sand is gathered from the desert – you will find patches of this unusual variety if you search for it at Saqqara.

Inside the pyramid, a furnace is lit and the sand is fiercely heated in a crucible for five days. It then becomes molten glass with special properties, and this is poured into cylindrical moulds. These are cooled slowly, and the tubes are filled with pure quartz crystals before they are sealed."

"I am sure, with your help, we can make some of these, but why does it have to be done inside the pyramid?" Sekhemkhet asked.

"You should know by now that special forces are at work inside these unique buildings," Neb-er-tcher replied. "This causes the crystalline structure of the rods to take on a unique shape, and it is what gives them their magical powers."

"Of course, I should have realised that the pyramids are places where wonderful things happen. But what are these objects used for?" the Pharaoh asked.

"They are called the 'Rods of Horus.' Those who keep them on their person will find that they impart energy, protect from disease, and maintain good mental and physical health."

Sekhemkhet could hardly contain his excitement. "Would we be able to make some of these in the Step Pyramid? I can ask for it to be unsealed so that we can enter. There are several unused antechambers and passages in there, so we would not have to disturb the sleeping Pharaoh Djoser."

"If you so wish, we can do that," the God of the Universe responded. "Just let me know when you have collected a quantity of the special sand, and some quartz crystals."

The Pharaoh was eager to close the meeting so he could make the necessary arrangements for the manufacture of these magical artefacts. All thoughts of what to do with the God of Darkness and the High Priest disappeared from his mind. The fact that he would soon possess some of the Rods of Horus, and enjoy the benefits they impart, dominated his thoughts.

But, whilst Sekhemkhet might have ceased to be preoccupied with the prisoner and his accomplice, at least for the time being, this was not the case elsewhere.

Chapter 16. The manufacture

"You fool," said Set. The ferocity of these words entering his mind startled the High Priest, just as he was starting to experience the soporific effects of a goblet of wine after his evening meal.

"This is Nebemakhet. Do you wish to speak with me?" he mouthed quietly, trying to curb his chagrin at the Evil One's opening comment.

"Yes, I do," came the reply. "Once again, my attempt to defeat Neb-er-tcher has failed due to your incompetence. Here I am, stuck in this miserable prison, probably facing execution, whilst you remain free."

The High Priest made a big effort to contain his initial urge to respond aggressively. The promised reward of being elevated to the gods was too great a prize to lose. Summoning all his powers to maintain a steady voice, he said: "It is indeed unfortunate that you have not yet been successful in your mission, but I have done all that you asked of me."

"In each case it was as if my attack had been anticipated. You must have been talking to other people about our plans," the God of Darkness replied, still displaying his anger.

"I can assure you that not one person has even been given a hint that we have spoken. After each of your attempts I have been summoned and questioned, but have never revealed any foreknowledge of what would happen. If I had been implicated myself, and arrested, you would have no other person on this earth to help you."

Whilst Set still needed to vent his aggression on someone, he had to accept Nebemakhet's statements at this time. He therefore suggested a different possibility. "If there has been no intentional breach of our secrecy, then there might have been an unintentional one."

"What do you mean by that?" the High Priest asked.

"I am talking about our conversations being overheard. When you talk to me, do you speak the words with your mouth as well as think them? Has somebody been listening at your door?"

"I doubt this is the case, because often I am alone in my own home. Perhaps your own transmissions have been detected, and there is only one individual who would be capable of doing this: your nephew."

After pausing to consider this possibility, Set had to concede that it was probably the most likely explanation. "Very well, in order to prevent this happening, you must come and stand by the wall of the jail where I am being incarcerated. If we are only a few metres apart, I can transmit my words very weakly so that only you will hear them. You will have to make sure that nobody is standing nearby."

"When would you wish me to come?" Nebemakhet asked, grateful that the one he regarded as a colleague may at last be acknowledging his contribution.

But the God of Darkness was displaying his irritation again. "That is a foolish question. If I told you that, the person who might be listening to us now will know when to try to intercept our conversation again. Instead, you must decide when to come. Stand next to the prison wall and call me; I shall hear you and reply."

Set then ended the discussion to reduce the opportunity for eavesdroppers, but it was already too late. Neb-er-tcher had been anticipating another transmission between the two villains but, having heard what they had just decided, realised that he would be unlikely to receive any further advanced warnings of an attack.

He considered his options. Firstly, he must remain alert to the possibility of an attempt being made on his life at any time. Secondly, he would try to ensure that there were soldiers nearby, or others who could provide help, whenever he went out of the palace. Thirdly, and perhaps most importantly, he would try and set a trap for his adversary, and thus remain in control of the situation rather than be a victim of it.

Should he discuss this latest development with Sekhemkhet? Following their most recent conversation, his opinion of him had changed a little. Was the Pharaoh becoming more preoccupied with enhancing his own glory, rather than doing what was best for his people? This seemed to be the way of earthlings, he mused. Even Imhotep had admitted that true altruism was still a distant goal in Egyptian society. Perhaps he would tell him – eventually – but he first needed to think how he could lure Set into a trap.

The Pharaoh was so eager to acquire the Rods of Horus, and enjoy the benefits they would bestow on him, that he could not resist telling everybody he met about them. The responses, whilst being respectful, did not always display the same level of enthusiasm. "Are you sure you need objects that possess such magical properties?" his wife, Djeseretnebti asked him. "They may bring you good health, but they could also have properties that are not meant for human beings."

"You are worrying unnecessarily, my dear," Sekhemkhet replied condescendingly. "Neb-er-tcher would not knowingly put me at risk. Remember also that, in my position, I have powers of my own and am an intermediary between the gods and the people."

Whilst this did little to allay her concerns, his wife realised it would be futile to try and persuade him to abandon the idea. General Intef also had reservations. "Your Majesty, these artefacts are inventions of a universe superior to ours. Our alien friends may be able to control them, but we do not know what damage they may cause to members of our own species."

"You speak just like Djeseretnebti!" Sekhemkhet replied in a mocking tone. "I had to remind her that, as both political and spiritual leader, I am watched over by our own gods, and they would not let any harm come to me."

Intef was still unsure of the wisdom of what had been arranged, but realised that the Pharaoh had already made up his mind. Rather than voice any further opposition, he simply responded: "I shall personally see to it that there will always be someone there to protect you, should you encounter any difficulties."

"Thank you, General; you are a very loyal subject. On your way out would you kindly ask one of the servants to summon the High Priest to come and see me."

Although Sekhemkhet had been warned that Nebemakhet was in league with Set, it did not inhibit him from wanting to boast about the magical rods he would soon possess. The Evil One was securely locked up now, so he would not be able to take advantage of any news that might come his way, officially or unofficially – or so he thought.

"The God of the Universe is going to demonstrate how to make rods that will give me magical and protective powers. I wish you to be present to learn how it is done, so that you will be able to manufacture some of our own once he has left us."

"How very interesting," the High Priest commented. "Do you have a date when this will take place?"

"Not yet, we first have to collect some crystals and special white sand, and then set up a furnace in the pyramid."

159

On hearing mention of the pyramid, Nebemakhet sharpened his attention. Opportunities for more mischief might just be presenting themselves. "Your Majesty, do you mean you are going to reopen the resting place of your late brother?"

"Yes," the Pharaoh replied. "There are several unused chambers and passages within the structure, and we shall carry out the procedure in one of those. If you are concerned about disturbance to the sanctity of Djoser's tomb, be assured that

this will not be my intention."

"I welcome your reassurance on that," the High Priest said. "But can you explain why the manufacture of these Rods must be carried out in the pyramid?"

"Although the first attempt to build a transmitter was not completely successful, it did allow the passage of the two aliens. Neb-er-tcher tells me that it is powerful enough to cause the molten ingredients to form a unique crystalline structure, and thus create its magical properties."

"It will be a privilege to witness what the God of the Universe does, and to learn how we can make these for ourselves," Nebemakhet commented. "Will we be joined by many others in the chamber?"

"I have not decided, but we shall need labourers for the furnace. The ingredients must be heated for five days, so the main witnesses will only need to be present at the start and finish of the procedure. When the final plans have been made, I shall notify all who should attend."

The High Priest was sure that what he had just heard would be useful to his evil associate, and resolved to inform him at the first opportunity. That same evening, he ventured out into the town and strolled past the prison where Set was being held. Many other people were enjoying the night air, now free from any worry of attack. At that time it would be too risky to stand next to the wall and attempt to make contact with his alien partner.

The situation on the second evening was much the same but, on the third, a rare shower of rain had kept others off the streets. Now was the opportunity he needed. He stood as close to the building as he could, and tried to keep in the shadows to escape notice should anyone decide to brave the elements. "Set," he said softly. "This is Nebemakhet. Can you hear me?"

Much to his surprise, the response entered straight into his mind even before he had the chance to call out a second time. "It is about time you contacted me. Are you sure nobody is listening to you this time?"

The High Priest resented the inference that he had carelessly allowed his previous conversations to be overheard, but restrained himself from commenting on it. "I am alone; nobody is in the vicinity. Something is going to happen that might be of use to us."

"I am listening. Tell me what it is."

"Neb-er-tcher is going make some Rods of Horus for the Pharaoh in the Step Pyramid. There may be an opportunity for another attack on him. Do you know anything about these Rods?"

The God of Darkness attempted a scornful laugh. "Of course I do. They were invented in my home universe by the God of the Sky. They can be dangerous in the hands of primitive species like earthlings."

Nebemakhet resented being regarded as a member of a 'primitive species,' and required a great effort not to respond with some equally disparaging remark. Confining himself to more practical matters, he said, "Do you wish take advantage of this situation to mount another attempt on the life of your nephew?"

After a pause, presumably to think the matter over, Set replied: "Yes, but you will have to help me escape from this prison. Is

Neb-er-tcher going to heat the ingredients in a crucible for five days? It is the way it is done in my universe."

"Yes, I have been told that, but little else about the process."

"Then the time for me to escape would be just before the process is complete. I could then enter the chamber shortly before the royal party. It will take a little time for my absence to be reported, and they will not want to abort the manufacture at this late stage. Hopefully there will be confusion, and guards will be diverted away from the pyramid to look for me in the town."

The High Priest was impressed by Set's plan, but there was one obvious question. "It remains to find a way to help you escape," he said.

"Am I the only one capable of thinking? You must obtain something with which to drug the guards. Put it in a vessel of wine, and take it to them when the time is right. Tell them that, as a holy man, you want to celebrate their success in capturing me. They will surely trust you, and accept the offer of a drink or two. When the drug has taken effect, I shall make my escape."

"There is an obvious choice of drug to put in the wine," Nebemakhet replied. "We have opium, which is used here to dull pain. When taken in larger quantities, and especially with alcohol, it makes a person lose consciousness."

"That sounds ideal," Set agreed. "After you have dealt with the guards, you must enter the pyramid with the other members of the party, before I escape, so as not to be implicated. But I expect you to influence the situation in the chamber so that I shall have my chance to attack. This time, there will have been no pre-warning, and I shall be victorious."

It was a busy time for all those who would be involved in the manufacture of the magical Rods. Sekhemkhet gave orders to his servants to go into the desert and collect quantities of the white sand and the quartz crystals. He personally visited the Step

Pyramid to select a suitable location for the operation, ensuring that it was a respectable distance from the resting place of his late brother.

General Intef was charged with finding a furnace and crucible. This was not an easy task, as they were only used for extracting the iron from fallen meteorites. Once they had been located, it was his responsibility to install them in the pyramid, and supply men to keep the fires burning for the required five days.

The High Priest had a different mission. He needed to acquire an adequate quantity of opium, without arousing any suspicion. When the dealer commented that it was unusual for a holy man to buy this drug, and especially such a large quantity, he replied: "This is for medicinal purposes. I have headaches every day, and just need a small amount each time so that I can continue my work serving the gods."

Neb-er-tcher had retired to his room to think carefully about what intrigue Nebemakhet and Set might be planning. He was sure they were not just abandoning any further attempt to kill him, but what opportunities were likely to be created that would give them the chance they were looking for? Moreover, his uncle was in prison, and could do no harm to anybody so long as he stayed there.

Eventually a possible scenario started to present itself. The manufacture of the Rods of Horus in the pyramid would be a suitable occasion where all parties would be present. Would the High Priest be able to help the Evil One to escape at that time? He would have to assume that this was probably what they were planning, even though he did not yet know how it would be accomplished.

Neb-er-tcher decided to do something he had not previously attempted since he came to Egypt. He would try to contact the Supreme God, Ra, in his own universe. To do this he would have to enter the Step Pyramid. Even though it was unreliable for transmitting people, its power would be needed to exchanges messages. No one was surprised when he arrived at the entrance to the tomb. It had been unsealed so that labourers could start work on installing the furnace, and the single guard stationed there was happy to let him pass.

Finding a quiet corner of the chamber, the God of the Universe settled himself down and silently began to project his message: "My Lord, Ra. This is your servant Neb-er-tcher. I am in the land of Egypt. Do you hear my voice?" He waited patiently, repeating his message every few minutes.

Eventually the reply came. "Yes, I can hear you. I have been trying to follow your progress in that land, but the images have sometimes been obstructed. We discovered that the God of Darkness followed you to your destination. Tell me what has been happening."

Neb-er-tcher briefly summarised the main events, including the attempts that have been made on his life, before coming to the main reason for his transmission. "I have reason to suspect that Set, with the aid of the local High Priest, will shortly mount another attack on me. It will take place in this pyramid, when I am demonstrating the manufacture of the Rods of Horus."

"I am surprised that you intend to trust these people with the secret of the Rods, but that is your decision," Ra replied. "What do you wish of me?"

"Although this transmitter is not reliable, for several more years it will be the only instrument we have to try and return Set to your universe. When the attack is made, if we both use our combined powers it may be sufficient to transmit him back into your care."

"I agree to try, and will be observing the situation in the pyramid when you are carrying out the procedure," the Supreme God said. "If we are successful, I shall deal with him, and then you will be

164

free to continue working for the good of the nation you have chosen to help."

When the day of the manufacture was announced, several plans were put into action. The Pharaoh had been successful in collecting the ingredients for the Rods, and had instructed General Intef to make sure the furnace would already be hot when the royal party arrived. Nebemakhet had prepared the mixture of wine and opium for the guards, and had spoken again with Set to tell him the date of the escape attempt.

Neb-er-tcher had requested a leather cloak to fit around his neck and cover up the top half of his body. He had said this would be necessary to protect him from the fierce heat of the fire, but he knew it would also make it difficult for the Evil One to stab him in his vulnerable areas, should the expected attack be made.

As Sekhemkhet entered the pyramid, he was like a child anticipating a new toy. He watched as the God of the Universe slowly added the white sand to the crucible, stirring it from time to time whilst uttering some incantations that the onlookers were unable to hear in their own language. Once he was satisfied, Neb-er-tcher announced that the process must now be left for five days to allow the crystalline structure of the flux to acquire the special properties. The furnace must be kept at maximum temperature during this time. As there was nothing more to see at this stage, the party dispersed and left the attendants to ensure that the fire continued to burn fiercely.

"Greetings, my friends," Nebemakhet said to the gaolers, as he entered the gates of the prison five days later. "I have come to thank you for guarding our special captive so efficiently. Has he given you any trouble?"

"No Sir," one of the guards replied, clearly pleased to receive this rare accolade from a senior member of the court. "He just

165

paces up and down, chirping away to himself, looking for any chance to escape. But we have the measure of him."

"Excellent. I have brought this flagon of wine for you to share. Enjoy it with my compliments."

"Sir, that is very kind of you. We shall keep it until the new shift comes on this evening, and let them enjoy a goblet or two with us."

Would this be too late to allow Set the opportunity to catch Neb-er-tcher whilst he was still in the pyramid? They had all been told to return to witness the last stage of the process just before sunset.

The day passed slowly for the Pharaoh, but soon he would actually be in possession of the Rods of Horus. He ushered the others into the chamber, eager for Neb-er-tcher to carry out the final stage of the manufacture, only to be told that this would take several hours.

"First I have to check that the flux is ready," the God of the Universe commentated. "Yes, I see that it is, so I shall now pour it into the clay moulds. Now we have to leave it until the material has cooled."

Sekhemkhet was starting to feel impatient. "Can we pour water over them to speed up the process?" he asked.

"Certainly not," came the reply. "It must cool naturally so that its structure can absorb the magical powers from the pyramid."

There was no alternative but to wait. By the time the moulds were ready for breaking, it was already dark outside. Several of the party had become bored, and wandered off to find places to sit down. The High Priest wondered if Set had managed to escape and enter the pyramid. The fading light would help him avoid being seen. Perhaps he was already hiding in one of the passages, observing what was going on in the chamber.

"We can now break open the moulds, add the quartz crystals to the rods, and then seal them," Neb-er-tcher at last announced, standing alone near the furnace. He picked up a stone to use as a hammer, and brought it down firmly on the clay.

Just as he did so, a figure darted out from a dark corner and tried to grab him. But his attack had been anticipated. Neb-er-tcher quickly turned and struck Set on the head with the stone he still held in his hand, knocking him to the floor.

Before any of the other bystanders could overcome their surprise and intervene, Nebemakhet rushed forward to help, realising that this would likely be the last opportunity to mount an attack. The Evil One struggled to his feet and grabbed hold of the High Priest, shrieking: "You fool, you have failed me again; you do not deserve to live."

"Now my Lord Ra; now is the time," The God of the Universe said, concentrating as hard as he could.

A blue light flickered over Set and Nebemakhet. Their images started to fade, but then returned. The High Priest was now locked in combat with the God of Darkness, venting his pent-up anger at being blamed for each failed attempt. The light returned, now stronger, and the image of the two brawling villains then faded rapidly until there was nothing left to be seen.

Had the High Priest finally achieved his wish to be transported to the home of the gods? The transmitter was unreliable, and they risked being damaged, both mentally and physically. Perhaps they never arrived at the other world, but were destined to remain lost in space, drifting between the parallel universes for all eternity.

Epilogue

Life in Memphis continued peacefully now that the danger of the God of Darkness had passed. Nebemakhet rapidly attained the reputation of a hero who had gone to his death trying to defend Neb-er-tcher from the attack by the Evil One. The few who knew the truth diplomatically kept it to themselves, if only to prevent it being said that the Pharaoh was harbouring a senior official whom he knew had been conspiring with the evil Set.

Sekhemkhet eventually took possession of the Rods of Horus, and continued to boast to everyone that he now had their magical powers. But he ignored the warnings he had been given not to abuse them, and only use them for good. After only seven years reign, he died. Once his body had been mummified, it was interred in the second pyramid, which was nearing completion. But construction then ceased before it could be used as a transmitter; the foundations subsided and the whole structure sunk into the sand. From then on it became known as the Buried Pyramid.

The faithful Imhotep outlived the Pharaoh by only a few years. He had devoted his remaining time to supervising the water conservation project that would ensure the farmers could still irrigate their crops during times of drought. On his death, his body was also preserved, and was buried in a secret tomb at Sakkara. In recognition of his untiring contribution to the nation, statues were erected in his honour – a privilege usually reserved only for pharaohs and gods.

As for Neb-er-tcher, he continued to advise successive pharaohs on the construction of pyramids that could permit gods to visit this earth. Complete success remained elusive until the seventh attempt, when the Great Pyramid at Giza was built by Pharaoh Khufu. This magnificent edifice was, and remains, perfect in every way. The God of the Universe, now nearing the end of his long life, used it to transmit himself back to his home.

Now that Neb-er-tcher demonstrated the new transmitter worked, other deities began to visit our world. And, it is said they still do.

Other novels, novellas and short story collections available from Stairwell Books. Scifi and Climate Change themed books are highlighted.

For further information please contact rose@stairwellbooks.com

www.stairwellbooks.co.uk
@stairwellbooks